2: LEAH DISCOVERS BOYS

Danny had been so kind to me. Twice he'd helped me out. Why had he done that? Surely Danny didn't fancy me…? Did he? I stared into space and a lovely feeling washed over me. A year-*eleven* boy fancied *me*! Wait till the girls found out.

"Leah, stop daydreaming. I don't know what's the matter with you today!"

It was Jan's voice, and not such a sympathetic tone this time.

"Sorry," I said, then I worked like a maniac until it was six o'clock and I was free to walk home with my lovely thoughts.

Also in the Café Club series by Ann Bryant

Have you read?
Go For It, Fen!

Look out for:
Luce and the Weird Kid
Jaimini and the Web of Lies

The CAFE Club

2: LEAH DISCOVERS BOYS

Ann Bryant

Hippo

Scholastic Children's Books,
Commonwealth House, 1–19 New Oxford Street,
London WC1A 1NU, UK
a division of Scholastic Ltd
London ~ New York ~ Toronto ~ Sydney ~ Auckland

First published by Scholastic Ltd, 1996

Copyright © Ann Bryant, 1996

ISBN 0 590 13425 6

Typeset by TW Typesetting, Midsomer Norton, Avon

Printed by Cox & Wyman Ltd, Reading, Berks.

For Mum and Dad

Chapter 1

Hi! My name's Leah.

My five good friends and I all live in a town called Cableden, and we go to school there, too. The one thing that the six of us girls have in common – apart from being thirteen years old – is that we all work in the same café. You're probably thinking that, one – it must be a very big café for all of us to work there, and two – we're very young to be working at all!

Let me start at the beginning with my friends. Fenella Brooks – Fen for short (the ambitious one) – has got an aunt called Jan who runs the café, and Fen managed to persuade Jan to let us work there after school on a rota basis. There are six of us and there are six working days of the week, so we work two hours a day each, and each week a different one of us gets to do Saturday. That makes it fair because there's an extra two hours' work on a Saturday, so more pay!

Right, that's what we all have in common. Otherwise we're quite different from each other. We don't look at life through the same eyes. I like that thought. I like to think that there's room on this earth for millions of different types of people.

Take me, Leah Bryan. They call me the musician. It's true I love music. I play the violin, the piano and the recorder. I'm in lots of music clubs and I enter music festivals and take exams. I also worry about everything.

I've told you a little about Fen. As well as being ambitious, she's single-minded and determined. She's very slim with brown hair that just touches her shoulders, and she usually wears leggings or jeans. Her best friend is called Natasha Johnston. We call her Tash for short. Tash (the peacemaker) is very kind and sensible. She's got lovely thick hair – lucky thing – and bright eyes. You'd call Tash "striking".

Then there's my best friend Andy Sorrell (the daring one). Andy is short for Agnès. That's a French name that you pronounce like this – Ann-yes. Andy's mother is French and her father is English. Andy is completely different from me. I don't dare to say boo to a goose most of the time, but I don't think there's anything that Andy wouldn't dare do. Even when she's afraid to do something, she makes herself do it. It takes a lot of guts to be like that. She's the smallest of us all with cropped dark hair and big brown eyes. My hair, by the way, is very fair and fine and hangs down almost to my waist, but I often wear it in a bun or a pony-tail.

Jaimini Riva (the brainy one) is really beautiful with very long black hair and coffee-coloured skin. Her father is black. He's a mixture of Ethiopian and Italian. Her mother is white. (You pronounce Jaimini Jay-m-nee, by the way.) I just know Jaimini will grow up to be a doctor or a surgeon or something like that.

Her best friend is Luce, short for Lucy Edmunson (the crazy one). It's fairly odd that those two should be best friends because Luce gets into trouble at school more than any of us. She's got a mass of wild, curly hair, half-way between blonde and auburn, green eyes and freckles. She's rather scatty, full of confidence and quite reckless. She loves clothes and jewellery and she's probably the noisiest of us all.

Right now Luce was peering in the jeweller's window and telling the rest of us which pairs of earrings she wished she could afford.

"That's nice," Jaimini said.

"What? Where?" Luce demanded, scanning the trays of sparkling silver and gold.

"That woman's coat," Jaimini said, and we all giggled as Luce realized we'd long since lost interest in her earrings, and while she was studying them with her nose pressed up against the window, *our* attention was on the passers-by.

"Thank you very much!" said Luce, going a bit pink under her freckles.

"It's a pleasure," answered Jaimini, tilting her head slightly and smiling broadly. I looked at my watch. Four o'clock.

"Help! I've got to get to work!"

It was my turn on duty at the café, and I felt a lovely feeling of pride as I said those words. It all sounded so grown up.

"Give Kevin a kiss from me," said Luce, with a wink.

"No fear," I told her, though really I would have loved to have given Kevin a kiss if I'd dared to – he is *so* good-looking.

"He's far too old to take any interest in a little thirteen-year-old like you," Andy told Luce, tut-tutting a bit.

"Oh, yes, he must be twenty-one at least. Positively ancient!" Luce agreed, sarcastically.

"You should be working, not eyeing up the chef," Fen told Luce.

Out of all of us it was Fen who was in charge, because it was she who had got the whole work thing started in the first place. I can't tell you the problems she had to deal with and the hurdles she had to overcome in order to get Jan and her parents to agree to the whole thing.

Andy had problems with her father, too. He was dead against the whole idea. He thought that she was too young and that her school work would suffer. He still doesn't realize that she's actually doing the job. Andy's mum is keeping it a secret because Andy's dad works in France and only comes home very occasionally for the weekend. I've only met him once and I found him quite scary. He stares at you with narrow piercing eyes and he uses sarcasm a lot. Right now, thank goodness, he's safely in France, but all the same we altered the whole rota to make sure that Andy is the last one to work on a Friday or a Saturday, just in case her dad pops home for another surprise weekend visit as he did once before.

"Good luck," Tash said to me, as I went round the back of the café to go in through the kitchen.

"I'll phone you later," Andy said.

"Work hard," Fen added. Poor Fen. Her mind is always on the café. She feels responsible for our Café Club. It's a good job she doesn't know what I've got lined up for the next week or so, I thought with a rush of anxiety. Ever since I'd started working at the café, music seemed so childish, and to make matters worse, I'd got two big events coming up. One is the Festival, which has nothing to do with school and the other is next week's dreaded school concert – the reason I keep having to go to practices and rehearsals at break times, lunchtimes and just about *all* the time!

I pushed open the door and the noise and bustle of the big, warm friendly kitchen surged up to meet me.

"Cheer up, it may never happen," Kevin quipped, as he pulled a massive tray of chips out of the oven, shook them vigorously and slid the tray back in. "Bet you've never seen that before," he went on as he turned a few beefburgers.

"What?" I asked as I hung up my coat, dumped my school bag in a corner and put on my apron.

"Chips that can do backflips."

"You're mad, Kevin!"

"Better than being gloomy and glum," he commented, with a significant look at my face. I smiled then because somehow Kevin always cheers you up. "Now let's watch you turn back to gloomy and glum when you see what I want you to wash up for me." He then dumped the fattiest, most revolting-looking frying pan you've ever seen into the washing-up bowl. I was studying all the little fat globules winking up at me, as Jan came in from the café.

"Hello, Leah. My goodness, is it four o'clock already? Can you go and clear tables three and six when you've done that?"

I set to work on the frying pan while Kevin, dipping his fingers in the washing-up and blowing frothy bubbles in the air, sang, to the tune of "Yesterday" by the Beatles, "Yesterday – all my bubbles seemed to float away!"

A couple of minutes later I hurried into the café and started clearing table three. I could hear some boys talking at the table behind me, and I could have sworn one of them said my name. Gathering crumbs, I inched round the table so I could see who the boys were. They were all from year eleven. One of them was Tash's brother, Danny, who's fifteen. I wasn't sure whether or not to say hello. If he had been on his own I would have done, but surrounded by his mates, I thought he might not want to speak to one of his little sister's friends, so I kept my head down as I piled up the tray. I could feel them all looking at me though and whispering, and I definitely heard my name mentioned again.

"Hello, Leah."

That made me look up in a hurry. I was just about to say, "Hi, Danny," when I realized it wasn't Danny who had spoken, it was one of the others.

"Hello," I mumbled, then went red because they were all grinning.

"Do you come here often?" the same voice

went on as the others smirked. I searched my mind for a clever answer but couldn't find one, so instead I very primly said, "I work here once a week actually and I would have thought Danny could have told you that, as his sister works here too."

That was quite a brave speech for me and my hands started to shake a bit from nervousness.

At that point Danny's voice cut in, "Shut up, Barker."

"Ooh, dear," said the boy called Barker in a really sarcastic voice, "are we defending our little friend, then?" That produced another smirk from the rest of the table but Danny looked uncomfortable. I picked up the tray and it was only then that I realized I'd piled everything up in one great tall pile, which was wobbling precariously. I was torn between preserving my dignity by trying to carry the tray through to the kitchen without dropping anything, or losing my dignity by putting it down and restacking everything in more manageable piles.

"Is this your first time clearing a table, Leah?" asked another grinning face from the hateful table. That did it. I'd show them! I'd carry that tray with its skyscraper of plates and bowls, and get into the kitchen without any accidents, if it killed me.

I took a couple of tentative steps, feeling my face turning hot and red.

"Oops, wobble wobble!" said another voice. My hands had begun to shake and it was true the pile was wobbling, which made me break out into a sweat. The next thing I heard was Danny's voice.

"Hey, did you hear that old Hawkenbury won eighty quid in the National Lottery?" he said. I immediately felt grateful to Danny for trying to divert their attention away from me.

"And talking of bets..." said the person called Barker, "a quid says Leah won't make it to the kitchen without dropping something."

I did a stupid thing then. I glanced up. It was only for a second, but nevertheless it was enough to make the plates rattle loudly. My glance told me that there were at least two other tables interested in watching my progress. And quite suddenly my face didn't feel red any more, it felt white. The pile was going to tip over, I felt certain.

"Come on, Leah," called out one of the boys, "see if you can get to the kitchen sometime today."

I felt sick because I can't bear it when I'm the centre of attention, even if I'm playing the piano or doing something well. This seemed like the worst moment of my life. I'd reached the swing door and I was dreading Jan or Becky coming speeding through and bashing into me, sending the contents of my tray smashing to the floor. I bit my lip and realized to my horror that I couldn't see where I was going because my eyes were blurred with tears. Then just when my arms were about to give way, the tray was suddenly magically removed from my hands. I looked up to see that my saviour was Danny – Tash's brother. I couldn't speak, not even to say thank you. Danny looked very confused himself, as though his feet had walked over to me and his hands had taken the tray without consulting him about the matter.

"Where shall I put it?" he mumbled.

I pushed open the kitchen door and nearly collided with Jan who was coming in to the café. Her eyes widened in surprise at the sight of one of the customers carrying a badly-loaded tray, while I stood pale and shaky at his side. Sizing up the situation quickly she flashed a brief smile at Danny and said, "Thank you, I'll take that now. Leah, you're needed in the kitchen." With that she turned on her heel, managing to keep the pile of plates rock steady without any apparent effort.

I followed her meekly through. Just before the door shut behind me I heard one of the boys say, "That's a quid you owe me, Barker," and then Barker's response in a loud complaining tone, "Nah, that's not fair, that isn't, she would have dropped the lot if it hadn't been for lover boy."

"What's going on, Leah?" Jan asked me as I scurried across to the dishwasher and started loading it.

"I made a mess of piling up the plates because of those boys making comments," I told her a little shamefacedly. She shook her head and tut-tutted once or twice, then put her hand on my arm and said, "Never mind, it's all good experience. You won't finish up with the leaning Tower of Pisa again, I bet!"

"Shouldn't listen to boys. They're full of fresh air," Kevin grinned through the steam and the smoke.

I didn't have to go back into the café till about ten minutes later when I went through the door very cautiously. Becky was just behind me.

"Come on Leah, hurry up," she said, trying to push past.

"Sorry, just checking there aren't any nasty year ten or eleven boys around," I said as I checked that Danny and his friends had definitely gone.

"Hold on, Leah," Becky said, looking me full in the face, "this is a café where you work. The chances are that all sorts of boys will come in here on a regular basis. You've got to get used to it, just say 'hi' to them like you would to anyone else, then get on with the job as though they're not there."

Becky was right, of course, but I knew I wasn't going to find it easy. I cleared the boys' table briskly and efficiently, all the time thinking, *You* just wait, next time you come in, you'll think I've been working here for years, I'll be so impressive. Then I started imagining all sort of clever retorts that I could have made to Barker and his mates. Not to Danny, though. Danny had been so kind to me. Twice he'd helped me out. Once, by diverting attention away from me – I blushed as I thought about it – and the other time by rescuing me when I was desperate.

Why had he done that? Why had they been talking about me in the first place? And what did Barker say just before I disappeared into the kitchen? "She would have dropped the lot if it hadn't been for lover boy." What did he mean by that? Surely Danny didn't fancy me…? Did he? I stared into space and a lovely feeling washed over me. A year-*eleven* boy fancied *me*! Wait till the girls found out. Perhaps Tash already knew. Perhaps Danny had made her swear not to tell me.

"Leah, stop daydreaming. I don't know what's the matter with you today!"

It was Jan's voice, and not such a sympathetic tone this time.

"Sorry," I said, then I worked like a maniac until it was six o'clock and I was free to walk home with my lovely thoughts.

When I got home, my sister Kim let me in. She's fifteen and very pretty. Her hair is long like mine, only thicker and a bit darker. She wears it loose all the time. She's very slim and looks great in jeans, which she was wearing on this day. I dumped down my school bag and flopped into a chair.

"Mum phoned. She's going to be a bit late. D'you want some cake?"

"Yes please, I'm starving."

"You look fed up," Kim commented.

She was right. My lovely thoughts about Danny had changed to horrible thoughts about the Music Festival that I was entering on Saturday. I would have much preferred to go down into town and see if Danny was in the café. If he was, he'd see a very different Leah from the last time he saw me. I'd get some advice from Luce and wear really trendy clothes and I'd definitely wear my hair down. People always complimented me when I had loose hair, but I was worried that it made me look too young.

"So why the long face?" Kim pressed me.

"Music Festival on Saturday," I answered briefly.

"So?"

She had opened her French homework and was jotting down a list of words.

"So, I'm not looking forward to sitting there for ages and ages and listening to the same piece being played over and over again. And neither am I looking forward to having Mum and Dad on one side and my piano teacher on the other side, all listening keenly to the adjudicator, noting everybody's marks, and desperately wanting me to win. Honestly

Kim, they want me to win more than I want to win myself. It's awful. And worst of all, I hate that terrible nervous feeling I get."

"I remember it well," said Kim, who had competed in lots of music festivals before she gave up all her music about a year before.

"I wish I could be ill on Saturday," I said, as the phone rang. "Hello?"

"Hi Leah, it's Fen. How did it go at the café?"

"Oh, fine," I said, deciding not to say anything about Danny yet, because I wanted to keep my special feelings all to myself for a little while.

"I don't suppose you're free to do the second half of my Saturday duty, are you? It's just that we're supposed to be going to my grandparents and I didn't realize we were setting off that early."

"That'll be fine," I said, doing a quick calculation. "I'll easily be back from the Music Festival by then."

"Great, you've saved my life."

As I put the phone down we heard Mum's

car pull in.

"Bet you anything Mum gets on to the subject of music within ten seconds of walking through that door," I said to Kim.

"Ten seconds?" squealed Kim. "You're joking! I'll give you 50p if she does."

"OK, and I'll give *you* 50p if it's more than ten seconds."

"Done."

The door opened. Kim looked at her watch.

Mum practically fell through the door with the weight of her shopping bags. We rushed to help her.

"Hello, you two. Pop the kettle on, Kim love. Did you both have a good day?"

"Not bad," Kim answered.

"Fine," I said.

"Homework?" she asked, taking off her coat and looking at the pad to see if there were any telephone messages.

"Done it," Kim said.

"Just about to do it," I said.

"Done your practice?" she asked, with her back to me.

"Not yet," I answered, raising my eyebrows significantly at Kim. She held up nine fingers to say nine seconds had gone by. I punched the air with my fist. Mum was quite oblivious of this silent communication between us. She looked a bit puzzled as Kim handed me 50p, but she didn't make any comment because her mind was obviously still on music.

"What have you been doing if you haven't been practising and you haven't done your homework yet?"

"I've been working at the café."

"Oh, Leah! I do think you've got a commitment to the piano with the Festival coming up so soon."

"I've also got a commitment to the café," I told her firmly as I picked up my school bag and went up to my room to do my homework.

Thirty minutes later there was a tap at my door and Dad's voice called, "Dinner, young lady."

"Hi, Dad. OK. I'll be down in a sec."

"Jolly good."

Dad, as you may have gathered, is quite an

old-fashioned sort of father. He often calls me young lady. He isn't being cold or posh. It's just his way. He's a mixture of quite shy, quite strict, quite funny, but *very* old-fashioned. He even smokes a pipe. When I was at primary school my friends used to come round specially to watch Dad sitting in front of the fire, smoking his pipe.

Andy once told me she loved being at my house because it made her feel Christmassy. I didn't know what she meant at the time, but now I know her family, I understand a bit. Her house is modern and bright, and your voice echoes in the hall with the polished wooden floor, and in the kitchen with the shining tiles. Our house seems softer and cosier. It's a bit like comparing a Barbie doll with an old patched teddy bear.

"Festival on Saturday," said Mum, beaming at us all over a steaming bowl of pasta. I didn't comment.

"Festival on Saturday, is it?" Dad asked rather absent-mindedly. He obviously wasn't concentrating because he knew perfectly well that it was the Festival on Saturday. We'd been talking about it for weeks in our family. Mum gave him an exasperated look and he just smiled back. Maybe he was winding her up. He did that sometimes. The phone rang again and Kim answered it this time.

"Hello."

Her eyes slotted into concentration mode and a look of extreme impatience came over her face. "I've told you I'm not interested," she snapped. "And in case you think I'm playing hard to get, I can assure you I'm not, so please don't phone again because you're wasting your time and mine."

With that she replaced the receiver and resumed eating her pasta as though she'd just got up to get a glass of water, not to deliver an ultimatum to some poor lovesick boy on the other end of the phone.

Kim is always getting phone calls from boys because she's so pretty and so natural. She never wears any make-up. She doesn't go in for trendy clothes either, but she still looks lovely, just in her jeans and T-shirt.

"I want to look like your sister," Luce sometimes wails at me as she desperately tries to flatten her hair down and smears vitamin E cream all over her face. "This should do it," she says. "If I do this every day, I should have porcelain skin and flat hair like Kim in a couple of years. And I think I'll take up running to get that long-legged athletic look."

"Forget it, Luce. Some people have got it, other just haven't," Jaimini says jokingly.

"It's OK for you," Luce answers. "You belong to the long straight hair brigade. I wish I did."

My mind came back to the matter in hand with Mum's next words. "Hurry up Leah, then you can get on with your practising."

I sighed and scowled.

"You *do* want to win, don't you?" Mum said, impatiently.

"No, Mum, *you* want me to win. My teacher wants me to win. *I* just want to get it over with."

Mum nearly choked on a mouthful of

spaghetti when I said that. She hastily gulped down some water, then said, "Jocelyn and David are coming on Saturday with Oliver, especially to hear you play." She broke into an enormous beam, obviously thinking this news would be the impetus to send me charging off to the piano to practise my heart out.

Jocelyn and David are friends of Mum and Dad. We met them three years ago when we were on holiday in Devon. Their son Oliver is a teeny bit older than me, and Mum and Dad think he's a really nice boy. We only see them about once a year and that's quite enough for me, because I have to "look after" Oliver, as Mum puts it. He wears glasses, has short hair, hardly says a thing, and when you *do* manage to drag the odd word out of him, he can't look you in the eyes.

Oliver's mum, Jocelyn, sort of "babies" him. No matter what Jocelyn is doing she can't help her eyes straying over to Oliver. She herself is tall and dignified-looking. Her hair is strangely puffed out round the sides and at the top, then taken back into what should be a bun or a French plait, but when you actually look at the back, there's nothing there. It just sort of ends. You can see the lacquer sparkling on it. I once discreetly touched it and it felt as stiff as cardboard.

David and Dad get on very well together because they're both rather vague. What usually happens is that Mum and Jocelyn get waist deep into an intense conversation about their children, while Dad and David talk in mumbles and grunts about nothing in particular.

"What time are they coming?" I asked, beginning to feel faintly uneasy. Mum kept her beam in place as she happily mapped out the day for me.

"We're meeting them at the Festival at ten-fifteen because the first class you're entering – the 'Under fourteens set piece' – is at ten-thirty. They'll also watch you in the 'Under sixteens set piece' and the 'Under sixteens open'. Then we thought we'd go and have lunch at Millers, because we loved that little restaurant last time, didn't we? Then we can have a wander round for a bit, before popping back here for a cup of tea and a chat. You can show them how your violin playing has come on since their last visit…" She paused and her eyes positively twinkled as she finished off triumphantly, "And in the evening we'll go back and watch the winners' concert. I'm sure you'll be in it, but even if you're not, we'll watch it anyway."

I'd quite forgotten about the evening. It's traditional at these music festivals to have a concert in the evening for the winners of all the classes which took place during the day. Great, I thought, sarcastically.

There was a short silence, then Kim coughed and said, "Oh, dear," with a faint smile.

"What do you mean, 'Oh, dear'?"

"I think Leah has made other arrangements, actually, Mum."

"What other arrangements?" Mum asked, her eyes narrowing.

"I'm supposed to be working at the café on Saturday afternoon from four o'clock."

"The café, eh?" Dad said, because he

obviously felt he ought to be joining in the conversation, but as often happens, he didn't quite know how to contribute. Dear old Dad. Mum ignored him.

"Leah," Mum began, in a voice that was sort of half whiny and half annoyed, but which I recognized as the tone that came before the real telling off... "Leah, I don't know how you can be so silly as to arrange work on such an important day – I mean, Saturday of all days..."

"It's not important to me, Mum. It's only important to you..."

"Let's put the telly on," Kim said, and Dad reached for the controls and switched it on before Mum and I could start another of our famous arguments that we seemed to have so often these days.

Chapter 2

The next morning at break-time the six of us were sitting in our favourite outdoor meeting place at school, down at the end of the netball courts. I was telling the rest of the girls about this great idea Kim had had the previous day.

"Kim reckons I ought to teach you all the recorder, then we could go to recorder club together and play in the school concert too. Miss Farrant would really appreciate another item for the concert I'm sure, and anyway I get fed up with doing so many music clubs and practices for the concert without you lot."

"At least we all do choir practice together," Jaimini reminded me.

"I think I'd be excellent at the recorder," Andy interrupted, enthusiastically.

"And very modest," Fen added, sarcastically.

"Come off it, Andy," Luce said, "you don't know the first thing about the recorder. You'd probably stick it in your ear!"

"Thank you very much," Andy said in a mock temper, and we all started to giggle.

"Yes, we'll all learn," Tash said brightly. "It'll be good fun. Then we could sing in the choir *and* play recorders in the concert."

"Right, we'll start in the dinner break," I announced.

"Where do we get the recorders from?" Jaimini asked.

"There are loads of spares in the music room," I told her. "Miss Farrant will be pleased to lend them out I'm sure, when she hears how keen we are."

As if on cue, the staffroom window was flung open and Miss Farrant stuck her head out.

"Is Leah Bryan down there?" she called, sounding more than a bit cross.

"Yes," I called back, jumping up.

"You were supposed to be at recorder practice, Leah," she snapped.

I clamped my hand over my mouth as I remembered. "Sorry," I called. "I just completely forgot about it."

"I hope you're not losing your sense of commitment, Leah, that's the second practice you've forgotten recently."

"Sorry," I said, again.

"Stop apologizing," Andy whispered, without moving her lips. Miss Farrant moved away from the window and I sat down feeling depressed.

"No wonder they call her Miss Ferret," Fen remarked. "They send ferrets down holes to sniff out rabbits and things, don't they?" I didn't answer. I was feeling too miserable.

"Cheer up, Leah," said Luce. "Just think, we could busk in the café when we get really good at the recorder."

Our groans were drowned by the bell for the end of morning break.

* * *

"No you may not!" snapped Miss Farrant, her right foot tapping the floor as it often did when she felt exasperated. "One – I don't lend out school property willy nilly, and two – you'd never get this lot to a standard where they could play a piece in time for the concert. And three – you've got enough on your plate at the moment without having extra coaching to do, Leah."

"We're not total beginners, Miss Ferret – Farrant," Andy pointed out. "It's just that we're all a bit rusty on reading music, that's all."

"I used to be able to play 'The Grand Old Duke Of York'," Luce added unhelpfully, "only our teacher was quite trendy and modern and…"

Miss Farrant's foot was tapping furiously, her arms were folded and her head tilted to one side. I saw Jaimini elbow Luce in the ribs. Poor Jaimini. She's perfected this action, having a best friend like Luce, who puts her foot in it all the time. Luce didn't get the message. She carried on to explain to Miss Farrant that her "trendy, modern teacher" had put the following words to the same tune…

"Oh, the Grand Old King of Nosh
He lived on sticky buns,
He put on weight the more he ate
Now he weighs ten thousand tons."

There was a horrible silence after that little anecdote from Luce, which would definitely win first prize for lack of tact. Even Luce suddenly realized she'd said something awful because underneath her freckles, a pinkness was slowly spreading over her face.

What I haven't told you is that Miss Farrant has a real weight problem. There is simply no way to describe her other than "fat". You couldn't say she was plump or heavily built – just plain fat. I know some people make fun of fat people, but Luce would never do that. She just wasn't thinking – as usual.

"Don't forget orchestra at lunchtime,

Leah," Miss Farrant said, coldly. With that she turned and went back into the staffroom. We just stood there.

"I've blown it with my big mouth," Luce said, in despairing tones.

"It doesn't matter. She probably wouldn't have changed her mind anyway."

"Poor thing," Jaimini said. "I'd hate to be fat like that." We were all nodding in agreement as a new lady emerged from the staffroom. She was chatting with Mr Osbourne, one of the science teachers.

She looked about thirty and very attractive. I don't mean pretty exactly. It was more that there was something that literally attracted you to look in her direction as though she were a magnet. She had really shiny hair like someone advertising a shampoo. She was slim and wore lovely fashionable clothes. In fact she was quite the opposite of poor Miss Farrant with her flat brown lace-ups and flabby face. Mr Osbourne and the new lady walked off down the corridor chatting like old friends. Perhaps they *were* old friends.

"Perhaps they're lovers," whispered Luce.

"Don't be silly," said Fen, sounding irritated. "Don't you know anything about body language? They haven't touched once."

"Could be a front," Luce pointed out. "In fact, my guess is that the moment they get in that lab they'll start passionately—"

"What are you girls doing clogging up the corridor? What lesson are you supposed to be in?"

"French."

"History."

"Tec."

It was a mixture of responses because we're not all in the same work groups.

"Well, off you go then," said Mrs O'Riley.

We all scattered obediently, but not before I saw something absolutely incredible. The new lady put her hand on Mr Osbourne's shoulder and gave him a quick kiss! I glanced round at the others to see if anyone else had spotted it. Luce had. We gave each other big-eyed "speak-to-you-later-about-that" looks, and off we all scurried.

"Listen, Leah," Andy said to me as soon as we were out of earshot of Mrs O'Riley, "we'll borrow the recorders anyway. Just for today, then we'll scrape together a few from Fen's sister and Luce's brothers, so we can return the school ones on Monday, and no one will be any the wiser."

"Oh Andy, what if we get found out? Miss Farrant specifically said we couldn't borrow them."

"Come on, Leah. Let's get them now, while Miss Farrant's still in the staffroom."

"I daren't Andy, it's too risky."

She didn't press me, but I knew she wouldn't leave it alone. This is what I was saying about Andy. This is how she got her reputation of being the "daring one". Once she gets an idea in her head, she *has* to carry it out, however dangerous or ridiculous it may be.

"Tell me where they are," she said urgently. I bit my lip. "Hurry up, Leah, we're both late already."

I blurted out where Miss Farrant kept the

recorders, added "good luck" and whizzed off to tec, as Andy zipped back along the now deserted corridor to go past the staffroom to the music room.

After a very quick lunch the six of us went down to the netball courts, with the recorders that Andy had managed to get from the music room stuffed up our jumpers. Unfortunately, there was a netball practice going on.

"Follow me," said Andy, so we veered off to the left.

Casting tons and tons of glances around us to check that we weren't being watched, we slipped further and further away until we were behind the huge hedge that marked the school boundary. We were, in effect, just out of bounds. Nobody ever came down here so we were quite safe. Also, the thick hedge would muffle the sound of our recorders.

The girls worked hard and I loved teaching them, but best of all was watching them when they played. It was so entertaining. Take Luce. Her shoulders go up and down. That's even funnier when you watch Jaimini beside her, with her eyebrows moving in time to Luce's shoulders! Fen had the habit of watching Tash's recorder out of the corner of her eye whenever she lost her place on the music. But what *she* didn't realize was that Tash was also watching *her* recorder because she'd lost her place. And on the end was Andy with her cheeks puffing in and out. It was hysterically funny, especially when the piece finished but Fen played another four bars because she'd managed to find her place, only it was the wrong place! We all burst out laughing and I told them how brilliant they were.

We were about to start the next piece when Jaimini glanced at her watch. "Oh, my stars!" she cried out. "Leah, your orchestra practice!"

"Oh, no!" I squealed, checking on my own watch. I was already ten minutes late. "Practise without me," I tossed over my shoulder as I ran as fast as I could towards the auditorium where orchestra practice took place.

I was practically outside the door when I

ran straight into the lady we'd seen with Mr Osbourne.

"My goodness, someone's in a tearing hurry," she said.

"I'm late for orchestra," I panted, "sorry."

With that I dived into the auditorium. The orchestra were playing away but they stopped at my dramatic entrance and all eyes turned on me which of course made me go red. If you push the auditorium door too hard it sticks open, and that's exactly what happened to me. Miss Farrant turned round from her place at the front of the orchestra and gave me a look that would have made a Christmas tree shed its needles.

"Sorry, I…"

"I'm getting just a bit tired of this, Leah Bryan," Miss Farrant cut in, in an ominously low voice. She was going to continue but another voice interrupted her from behind me.

"I'm so very sorry about Leah, Miss Farrant. It's my fault she's late. She was showing me where things are. I do hope her absence hasn't spoilt your rehearsal."

It was that lady again. I turned round and stared at her wide-eyed.

"Thank you, Leah," she said with a quick smile at me.

"That's OK, Mrs..."

"Merle," she whispered.

"Mrs Merle," I stammered.

"Right you are," said Miss Farrant rather stiffly, with an attempt at a smile at my saviour, but it came out as a sort of grimace. "Go to your place, Leah, so we can get on with the rehearsal."

Orchestra seemed to be over in no time at all, mainly because my mind kept wandering off. The girls were waiting for me in the corridor looking very despondent.

"What's the matter?" I asked them.

"We can't do it properly without you," Andy said.

"So we're having a practice tonight at my place," Tash said.

"After Jaimini's finished work – six-fifteen. Is that OK?"

"Yeah, fine," I said, trying to disguise my

sudden high spirits. That meant I would see Danny again. Great! I hadn't told the others about what happened in the café because it somehow seemed too personal. I'd been going round hugging secret thoughts about Danny to myself, and now it seemed as though fate was trying to push us together. I couldn't wait for six-fifteen to arrive, and yet I was also rather nervous about it.

"Where are the recorders?" I asked.

"We've left them in the hedge for now. We thought they'd be safest there, and we can pick them up after school."

"Hey, we've got that new teacher," Jaimini reminded us. "Mrs Merle, she's called. She's the new PSE teacher."

So I told them all about how Mrs Merle had saved me from the wrath of Miss Farrant, and they listened open-mouthed with amazement.

As always happens with a new teacher, the class sat perfectly still and silent while Mrs Merle began to talk. It wasn't that we were trying to make a good impression, just that we wanted to size her up – see how she scored on a scale of one to ten for strictness, sense of humour, homework, making the lesson interesting etc. After less than five minutes I'd given her ten for everything. Andy slipped me a note which said exactly the same thing.

Imagine my horror when this lovely, quiet, interesting lesson was interrupted by the door opening. All eyes flew to the door and I gasped to see Miss Farrant standing there, quivering with rage and holding – yes you guessed it – our recorders.

"Excuse me interrupting, Mrs Merle," she began coldly, "but I wonder if I may have a word with some of the girls in here."

Mrs Merle must have nodded or something because Miss Farrant continued, "Leah Bryan, did I or did I not expressly deny you permission to borrow six recorders?"

"Yes," I managed to whisper.

"So could you explain why these six school recorders have just been handed in by a passer-by – a complete stranger, who apparently found them stuffed in a hedge *outside* the school premises?"

"It was my fault," Andy answered before I could utter a word.

"And mine," I said, to be fair.

The others must have had the same thought – that we were all in this together – because one by one they all added, "And mine".

The rest of the class were riveted by this conversation. It must have been better than any drama lesson.

"We were practising something for the concert, you see," Jaimini tried, but Miss Farrant's stony face didn't move a muscle.

"It was going to be a surprise," Luce said.

"And there was netball practice going on, so we had to go somewhere else..." Tash continued.

"That was the only place we could think of," Fen finished off, "...or it wouldn't have been a surprise if you'd heard us practising."

Still no sign of the stone cracking. This time it looked as though we'd *really* done it. There was nothing for it but to wait quietly to hear the verdict.

"Did it not occur to you that the recorders might have been stolen, rather than handed in?" Andy shifted uncomfortably in her seat. One of the boys sniggered. "But worse – *far* worse than that – is the fact that you blatantly took these recorders when I had quite expressly forbidden you to do so. So … detention after school today, ten to four, auditorium, all six of you."

With that she turned on her heel, leaving the PSE lesson with a great gash down the middle of it. I've no idea what Mrs Merle talked about after that. I wasn't listening. The others had sunk back in their chairs too, apart from Jaimini who was sitting with her shoulders hunched and her face in a frown. No wonder. It was Jaimini's turn at the café. She couldn't miss it and yet she couldn't miss detention either. What a hopeless situation. My high spirits had sunk to ground floor level.

At ten to four, five of us sat in the auditorium,

pale and anxious. Jaimini had decided to go to work at the café and just pretend she forgot about the detention. If questioned, the rest of us could quite honestly say we hadn't seen her since PSE because she was in different work groups for the rest of the afternoon.

Miss Farrant sat stony-faced, having told us to write out a hundred times, "I must not take school property without permission." When I'd filled half a sheet she suddenly said, "Wait a minute…"

We all looked as innocent as possible. This was the moment we'd been dreading. "There were six of you earlier on, and I see only five. Where's the other girl?"

We made a big thing of looking round and appearing very surprised.

"Oh, it's Jaimini," said Tash thoughtfully to the rest of us, as though she'd only just worked it out.

"Oh, yes," we answered with concerned looks.

"She must have forgotten," Luce remarked with an anxious edge to her voice.

"I've not seen her all afternoon. She's not in my group, you see," Fen offered helpfully. The rest of us shook our heads and murmured, "No, neither have I." How we managed not to smile, I don't know. Miss Farrant walked amongst us as though we were hiding Jaimini in our pockets or something. It's not for nothing she's nicknamed Ferret!

"I'll see that girl on Monday. I think there's more to this than meets the eye. If I find out that you're all in this together, there will be far reaching consequences, I can assure you."

Looking terrified we got straight back to work. My head was the last to go down which meant I was the only one to see the ghost of Jaimini gesticulating at me through the little square window in the door. It had to be a ghost because the real Jaimini should have been at the café by now. I glanced back at the clock on the wall. It was nearly four o'clock. Miss Farrant was marking books. Getting over my shock I realized that it was actually Luce's attention that Jaimini was trying to attract, but Luce was deep into her lines, and just out of jabbing-in-the-back distance. I didn't want Miss Farrant to notice anything amiss so I tore off a tiny corner of my sheet and wrote on it "Jaimini at door". Then I put my hand up.

"Yes," said Miss Farrant, when I coughed.

"May I go to the loo, please?"

"Go on, then. Be quick," was the brisk answer. As I went past Luce I discreetly dropped the little piece of paper on to her desk. Safely on the other side of the door with Jaimini we watched as Luce read the note, then looked in our direction. "Be careful, Luce," I whispered under my breath. "Don't get caught whatever you do."

A moment later Luce had joined us. "I said I was going to the loo, too. But what's up, Jaimes? Why aren't you at the café?"

"I've lost my purse. It had that ten pound note in it... I'm supposed to pick up some stuff from the chemist for Mum. I promised I'd get it on my way to the café. She'll kill me if I go home without it. Then I remembered that you said something about knowing where you could get some money from without any problem, Luce…?"

Luce frowned in concentration.

"Something to do with what you and Leah saw…?"

"Oh, yes," Luce answered, the puzzled look slipping away. "Leah and I actually saw Mrs Merle and Mr Osbourne kissing!"

Jaimini gasped. "What, properly?" she asked in wonder.

"It was a peck on the cheek, Luce," I put in. "Anyway, what's that got to do with ten pounds?"

As soon as I'd asked I knew the answer. "Luce!" I squealed. "You're not thinking of asking Mrs Merle for ten pounds hush money, are you?"

"Well…" Luce began, looking a bit sheepish.

And that was the moment that we got caught. The door opened and Miss Farrant, with a face like thunder, gave us her meanest stare.

"You're late, Jaimini," she said finally, her voice dangerously quiet.

"I ... I..."

"Yes...?"

"I'm sorry."

"We'll add ten minutes on to the end to make up for it. I don't think your friends are going to be very happy."

She then held the door for us, and because there was nothing else we could do, we went in. The others were all looking like rabbits startled in the headlights. They didn't know what was going on. Never before had I seen so many anxious, questioning, darting eyes in one room. Fen had gone very pale. I saw her look at the clock. Jaimini, looking absolutely distraught, mouthed "sorry" to Fen and sat down heavily.

When it came to the café, as I've already explained, Fen felt responsible. Her hand shot up immediately.

"May I go to the loo please, Miss Farrant?"

The look that Miss Farrant gave her was rather like the look you'd give someone who'd just told a really rude joke that you didn't approve of. "You'd better be quick about it.

We don't want any more trouble, do we?" she said in an unpleasant sarcastic tone. I suppose it was no wonder that she was suspicious. After all this was the third person to want to go to the loo.

Fen hurried out. From where I was sitting I could just about see what we call the "gap in the hedge" which was one of the exits from the school, like a little short cut. With a careful eye on Miss Farrant, I kept watch on the gap in the hedge. Just as I thought, after less than a minute, Fen bolted through at top speed. Andy's eyes met mine, large and fearful. She had been watching out, too. I began to feel sick on Fen's behalf. She was going to be in big trouble.

When five minutes had gone by and there was still no sign of her return, my stomach started feeling like a washing-machine. Miss Farrant hadn't said a single word since Fen left the room, and her silence seemed twice as deadly as her harshest words. I could hardly bear it and neither could the others, especially Jaimini who was nearly in tears.

"You may go now. Bring me your papers, please."

At last.

We deposited our papers on her desk and managed to leave the room in a controlled fashion, expecting at any moment that Miss Farrant would change her mind and make us stay for another half hour. Still she made no comment at all about Fen's unexplained absence.

Once safely away from the auditorium we charged out of school as fast as we could. By some silent agreement we didn't say a word to each other until we were safely through the gap in the hedge, then the words tumbled out frantically.

Chapter 3

"It's all my fault," Jaimini said. "You couldn't help it."

"It was *my* fault. She must have heard me squeal at Luce outside the door," I said.

"That means it was my fault for making you squeal," wailed Luce.

"Shut up!"

That was Andy. She was cross. "Who cares whose fault it was. What about Fen? She must be at the café."

"She's going to be in *big* trouble," Tash said, biting her thumb.

"We're not going to let her carry the can on her own. We're going to share the consequences of this. It's nobody's fault."

Andy was in her most decisive mood. The rest of us nodded and waited to hear what she would say next.

"I'm going to the café. Coming?"

Again we all nodded.

"Scouts' pace," Andy added with her usual economy of words.

"What's that?" Luce asked.

"Twenty walks, twenty runs. Let's go."

We passed quite a few people but we didn't care what we looked like. We kept the rhythm going all the way, and we weren't at all puffed out when we got there.

"Front entrance or back?" Andy asked us over her shoulder.

She had reached the front and was glancing in through the huge picture windows.

"Whoops!" she suddenly said, whacking me in the stomach as she backed out of view of the window and made urgent swipes at the air to get the others back.

"Guess who's in the café?" she went on, not really expecting us to guess. "Mrs Merle and Mr Osbourne!"

Luce gasped and turned to me. "You see, I was right. They're lovers."

The others were looking very puzzled. "Just ignore her," I told them.

"Let's go round the back. I want to see Fen," Tash said. We followed her round and slipped in through the back door.

"No, girls, no!" came Kevin the chef's voice. He held his hands out in front of his face as though protecting himself from hundreds of screaming fans. "Don't swamp me, girls. I know I'm wonderful, but you must try and leave me alone!"

We couldn't help laughing at his ridiculous sense of humour. You don't imagine a chef to look like Kevin. He's extremely fit because of all the running and training in the gym that he does during his time off. He works very hard and takes his job seriously, even though he jokes about everything else. Jan reckons he's the best chef in England, but she doesn't like to tell him too often in case he leaves and goes to work at a posh hotel somewhere.

"Is Fen here?" Tash asked him, trying not

to giggle.

Kevin made a big thing of peering into the washing-up. He parted the frothy bubbles on the top and bent over.

"Nope. Can't see her," he announced.

At that moment she walked in from the café carrying a tray of dishes, and we fell on her like a pack of ravening wolves.

"Oh, Fen, you're so brave," Tash said.

"I'm really sorry Fen … it was my fault…" Jaimini said.

"No, it was *my* fault," I said.

"No, it was *my* fault," Luce insisted.

"Here we go again," Andy said. "Don't worry Fen, we're all going to share the punishment."

"What *is* the punishment?" Fen asked fearfully, as she steered a path through us, and unloaded her tray into the washing-up.

"We don't know. Old Ferret-features is playing a new game and we can't fathom it out," Andy told her. "She never said a single word when you didn't come back. She didn't even *look* a single word!"

"Uh-oh." From Kevin's direction.

We turned to see if he'd dropped something or burnt something.

"What?"

"Fen's in trouble twice," he said, without looking round. Then he tossed a pancake nearly to the ceiling as he said, "Once with Ferret-features, whoever she may be..." Then he tossed another pancake even higher than the first as he said, "And once with Jan!"

At that moment Jan walked in. She was not a happy lady.

"Is this great deputation supposed to make up for the fact that I had nobody for the first half hour?" she asked.

"It's my fault," Jaimini said. "I'm really sorry."

"No, it was *my* fault," I said. "*I'm* really sorry."

"No, it was *my* fault," Luce said, with even more emphasis, "and *I'm* really sorry." Then a high girly voice from the direction of the Aga said, "Noo, noo, noo! It was *my* fault and I'm sorrier than any of you, so nur nur!"

Even Jan laughed at that, but Jaimini was clutching her arm and desperately trying to make a proper apology. Jan covered Jaimini's hand with her own and said, "Don't worry. It sounds as though you've got a particularly difficult music teacher, from what Fen tells me. I've already given Fen a rocket, and I'll just say to the rest of you, do *not* let this happen again. You can't take *any* risks at school. You have to be on your best behaviour all the time, if you want to hang on to this job. Got it?"

We all nodded.

"Right. Enough said. Now, either go and sit in the café and have a drink, or go along home. Either way I want you out of this kitchen."

Jan was back to normal. She's a very fair, kind person, but she won't stand any nonsense. Fen's lucky to have her for an aunt. While she's in the café, though, Jan has stressed that Fen is on equal terms with any other employee. In a way, Fen gets it even tougher, because Jan is so intent on making sure that she's not favouring her niece. I bet

Jan really laid into Fen earlier on when she turned up late instead of Jaimini.

"Let's have a Coke. I'm dying of thirst," Luce said. "Come on."

"No wait..." Fen said, but Luce had already pushed her way through the swing door into the café and we were all following. Immediately it became clear what Fen was about to say. We'd all forgotten about Mrs Merle and Mr Osbourne sitting cosily at a corner table for two.

"Pretend you've not seen them," hissed Luce, turning round to the rest of us. So we all concentrated hard on looking at Luce to see which table she was heading towards. Luce, typically, however, couldn't keep her eyes off the corner table and subsequently walked right into a chair and knocked it over which caused everyone in the café, including Mrs Merle and Mr Osbourne, to turn round.

Heaving the chair back on to its legs, Luce went bright red. Andy plunged on ahead and sat down at a table for six, the rest of us close behind. Luce was the last to sit down. You won't believe this, but she was *still* staring at the corner table.

"Sit down," Andy hissed, as Jaimini yanked on her friend's hand and Luce toppled awkwardly into her chair. Mrs Merle gave us a little wave and called over, "Hello, girls."

"Hello," we all called back, except Luce, who waved vigorously and said, "Hello, Mrs Merle and Mr Osbourne," then grinned at them like a Cheshire cat, until a severe elbow in the ribs from Tash made her turn her attention back to us.

"Let's listen to what they're saying," whispered Luce conspiratorially.

"That's impossible unless we're totally silent ourselves," Jaimini pointed out.

"That's no problem," Luce said lightly, her eyes already straying back to the corner table.

"Do try and keep your friend under control, Jaimini," I said jokingly, as Fen came over to us.

"I'm allowed to take your order, so please try and give it to me sensibly," she said, pen poised over her pad.

Normally we weren't allowed to take orders or take food to the tables. We mainly had to do washing up and clearing up, so this was exceptional.

"We all want Cokes, don't we?" Andy said looking round.

"Chocolate milkshake for me, please," Luce said.

"Everybody else, Cokes?" Fen confirmed, writing it down. Then she leant over and as we moved in to hear better, she whispered, "Let's ask Mrs Merle if she could fix it for us to play our piece in assembly on Monday. That might put Ferret-features in a better mood. Maybe when she hears how good it is, she'll think twice about laying on even more punishment."

"Good thinking," I said. "Who's going to ask her?"

"One of you lot because I'm going to get your drinks," Fen told us.

Luce's eyes couldn't help straying over to Mrs Merle and Mr Osbourne.

"Fancy a good-looking woman like Mrs

Merle fancying a boring middle-aged man like Mr Osbourne," she commented a little too loudly. "He's not exactly good-looking, is he?"

We all urgently shushed her while casting surreptitious glances over to the corner table to see if Luce's unfortunate observation had been heard. It had. Mrs Merle nodded and smiled and Mr Osbourne got up.

"You idiot, Luce. See what you've done now," Andy whispered loudly.

We all sat still as statues, waiting for Mr Osbourne to tell us to mind our own business or something. He seemed to be taking an awfully long time reaching our table. I turned round slowly to see where he'd got to, only to discover he was nowhere in sight, but Mrs Merle was at the till paying. I must have been staring at her, because she smiled at me, rolled her eyes and said, "Men! Never got any money!" before heading for the door.

"Oh, that reminds me. What am I going to do about that ten-pound note?" Jaimini exclaimed, but nobody paid any attention to poor old Jaimes because we were more concerned about not letting Mrs Merle go.

"Stop her, quick!"

It was Tash who jumped up.

"'Scuse me, Mrs Merle, but may we possibly have a quick word with you?"

Mrs Merle looked rather taken aback, but came to our table and sat down at the spare place.

"Did I hear something about ten pounds? Is that the problem?" she asked, looking concerned.

"Yes," Jaimini answered quickly. "I've lost ten pounds from my pocket. I promised Mum I'd get her something from the chemist, but when I looked for the money, I saw it had gone."

"Well, just this once I'll lend you the money, but I want you to pay me back as soon as possible."

"Yes, of course," said Jaimini, sounding very relieved. "Thank you very much."

"You ought to report it to your class tutor, you know."

"Yes, I will on Monday," Jaimini assured her, then she said, "I'd better go now." Fen was at the table with the drinks and Jaimini softly said, "Whatever punishment you get, Fen, I'm sharing it, OK?" Fen smiled and said, "Thanks, Jaimes. See you later."

"I thought you'd had your punishment," Mrs Merle said as Jaimini left the café.

"Well, that's really what we wanted to talk to you about," I said, "and it's a long story…"

"In that case I'd better order another cup of coffee from this nice young waitress," Mrs Merle said brightly as she sat down in Jaimini's chair.

Andy, Tash, Luce and I then took turns in the telling of the detention saga and then Fen's idea about the recorders.

"So you want me to persuade Miss Farrant to let you play your piece on Monday in assembly?" Mrs Merle summarized at the end.

"Yes please, and could we pretend it was your idea?" Luce asked.

There was a small silence while Mrs Merle frowned, deep in thought, then she suddenly said, "OK, we'll give it a whirl."

"Oh, great!" we all said with relief. Luce clapped her hands delightedly. "Well, it can't make things any worse, can it?"

Mrs Merle suddenly looked very serious and preoccupied as she said, "I, er, I wouldn't have thought so." Then she changed back into her brisk fast gear and said, "Right, I'd better be making a move."

She left her money on the table and moved to the door as we thanked her profusely. When she was almost out of the door she changed her mind and came back to our table.

"Don't be too hard on Miss Farrant. She can't help the way she is … at the moment." Then she turned and went, leaving us staring after her.

A few minutes later we paid Becky and went out through the kitchen.

"Bye Jan, bye Fen."

"See you later everybody," Fen said. "I'll bring Rachel's recorders by the way. She's got two."

"And I'll bring Tim's and Leo's. I think they've got three," Luce added.

"And I've got my own, so that makes six," I summed up. Then my stomach did a quick somersault at the thought of seeing Danny later.

At six-fifteen that evening we all turned up at Tash's. Unbelievably, it was Danny who opened the door to me. I tried to look casual and said, "Hi," in a nonchalant voice and added, "How are you?" which I realized sounded stupid the moment I'd said it.

"OK," he mumbled, eyes down.

"Thanks for … helping me out yesterday, Danny."

"That's OK."

"I hate to think what would have happened if…"

"That's OK."

I wondered whether he was always this shy or whether it was me making him tongue-tied. I flashed him my best smile, hoping he might relax.

"Tash and the others are upstairs," he managed, before bolting off into the sitting room.

Tash was surprised to see me. "I didn't hear you ring," she said.

"Danny let me in."

"Most unusual for Danny!"

I quickly changed the subject before anyone made any comments or I went red.

"Have we got enough recorders? And was it really that bad at lunchtime?" I asked them as I joined their circle on the floor and got presented with a glass of lemonade by Tash.

"Recorders courtesy of my brothers and Fen's sister," answered Luce, "and yes, we were the pits. We lost our places, forgot how to play half the notes you taught us and couldn't keep together. It was awful."

So for ten minutes we went right back to scratch and I counted like mad to keep them in time. We were right in the middle of "Morning Has Broken" when Tash suddenly said, "I think Danny fancies you, Leah."

"What!" I screeched, trying to look suitably

horrified, while the others leaned forward, eager for further explanation from Tash.

"Before you all came, when I warned him that there would be an awful racket in here after six-fifteen, he groaned and said, 'Oh, spare me,' then about five minutes later he asked me casually which of my friends were coming. I reeled off your names. He was drawing a map for geography at the time, and I noticed that he didn't react to any name except yours, Leah. When I finished off 'and Leah Bryan' he looked up from his map and was about to say something, but didn't. Instead he went a bit pink and got back to his geography very vigorously."

"Well, that doesn't prove a thing," I said, so that no one would guess how happy I felt. "Come on, let's get on with this." I handed each of them an A4 sheet.

"What's this?" Jaimini asked as they all studied their papers, the matter of Danny thankfully forgotten.

"I made up the tune a few weeks ago and I quickly added the other two parts just now," I told them.

"You clever thing," Andy said, squeezing my shoulder in a special Andy gesture.

"It's a piece for all six of us to play. Andy and I are part one, Luce and Jaimini, part two, and Tash and Fen, part three."

"And Peta, part four," came a squeaky little voice from outside the door.

"And Peta in the bath more like," came Tash's mum's firm voice. This was followed by four loud blasts on a very squeaky-sounding recorder.

"Go away Peta, we're busy," called Tash through the door, while the rest of us tried to stifle our giggles. Peta is Tash's only-just-three-year-old sister. She's very cute, though Tash describes her as a real handful.

"Let her come in, Tash," pleaded Fen. "Just for a moment." There was a loud knock at the door at that point which was quite obviously made by the recorder and not Peta's hand.

"You'll break it," Tash called out warningly.

It was a strange throaty voice that replied, "Little pig, little pig, let me come in."

Fen rocked backwards and forwards help-less with stifled mirth at little Peta's imitation of the big bad wolf.

"Not by the hair on my chinny chin chin," Luce played along with a wink for us.

"Then I'll huff and I'll puff and I'll blow your house in," came the fierce response. This was followed by silence. We all strained to listen for the huffing and puffing but because there wasn't a single sound we assumed Peta must have gone. "Just check whether she's still there," Fen begged Tash.

When Tash reluctantly opened the door, we had a job holding back our amusement. There stood little Peta, wearing absolutely nothing, clutching her little plastic recorder and going red in the face with the effort of blowing. The amount of puff coming out of her mouth however, would scarcely have been enough to disturb a candle flame. When she saw us all, a huge beam spread over her face. She made a beeline for Fen who she knew the best.

"Hi, Fenny Penny," she said.

"How's my favourite two-year-old?" Fen

asked, knowing very well that Peta had just had a birthday, but trying to get a reaction.

"I fink your favert two rold is living in annuver person's house, cos it's not what I am, cos I am…" She blasted hard on her recorder and proclaimed, "ONE!" at the top of her voice. Another blast was followed by, "TWO!" in a screech, and a final blast heralded the triumphant great squawk, "FREEEEEEEE!"

"Be quiet Peta, you'll hurt your voice," Tash said sternly. "She's showing off," she added quietly to us. We knew she was but we liked it.

"You are supposed to be in the bath, young lady," said Tash's mum, sweeping in and scooping Peta up in her arms. Peta immediately scrambled and kicked to try and escape, then suddenly went rigid and anxiously asked her mum, "Will I break my voice if I shout?"

"You won't break it, you'll just hurt it," Mrs Johnston answered.

"Good," Peta said, nestling into her mum, "because Danny's voice broke and now he talks like this…" She pressed her chin into her chest and frowned heavily as though to make everything as low as possible, then in a peculiar growl she said, "OK, who dropped one?"

Well, you can imagine the effect that had on us. We collapsed into laughter. Mrs Johnston tried hard not to laugh. "That's enough, Peta," she said. But Peta was thoroughly enjoying playing to the gallery. "Don't talk crap," she said to her mother, still in the low growl.

"You do *not* say that!" Mrs Johnston said in a loud shocked voice, while the rest of us desperately tried to stop laughing.

"Danny does," came the innocent reply.

"I don't think you can have heard him properly," Mrs Johnston tactfully suggested.

"I *did* hear him proper," Peta assured her mum with wide eyes and a series of vigorous nods.

"Even so, little girls must never talk like that, Peta. Do you understand?"

"Yes, Mummy Dummy."

Mrs Johnston obviously decided to let that

one go. "Come on, bath," she said briskly. "Say night night to Tash and her friends."

"Ni night, Tasher Basher."

"Ni night."

"Ni night, Fenny Penny."

"Ni night, Peta."

"Ni night, Andy Pandy."

Gales of laughter all round.

"Ni night, Loosey Goosey."

More gales of laughter.

"Ni night, Leah Peah."

Hysteria.

"Please don't encourage her, girls," from Mrs Johnston. "She's bad enough without an audience." And Peta skipped out.

"What about Jaimini?"

Peta turned and stared at Jaimini for a few seconds then said in reverent tones, "Ni night, Janey Bootiful."

"Ah, isn't that sweet, Jaimes?" said Luce affectionately to her friend.

"Ni night, Peta," Jaimini smiled, blowing her a kiss. Mrs Johnston shut the door but we could still hear their departing voices.

"Janey Bootiful blew a kiss to me. Do you know where it landed? On my chest button." We turned back still grinning into our circle.

"She's so sweet, Tash," said Luce. "I wish I'd got a sister living with me instead of two brothers."

Luce lives with her mum and stepdad, and goes to visit her real dad every so often. She's got two stepbrothers, who are grown up and only visit occasionally, and twin half-brothers, from her mum and stepdad. Her real dad and his new wife have got a little boy and a little girl.

"Let's get back to work. I've got to go in a few minutes," Andy said, changing the subject. So for fifteen minutes we worked hard on the piece I had made up for them. It sounded better than I'd thought it would.

"Right, you just need to practise it a bit, then it'll be ready for Monday. With any luck we might get to play it in the school concert."

"She *will* be pleased, won't she?" Tash asked sounding a little dubious and anxious.

"Let's hope so," I said, picturing Miss

Farrant with that cross look, sitting at the front of the auditorium. My picture was broken by the loud ringing of the phone.

"It's for Jaimini," Danny said through the door. He brought the phone in for her and hovered while she spoke to her mum.

"Yes … I was just coming … yes … hold on a sec…" Then to us, "Mum says Dad doesn't mind running us home as it's dark."

"I'll walk," Fen said. "I've got a torch and it's not far."

"Me too," I said.

As Jaimini told her mum that Luce and Andy could do with a lift, Danny turned nonchalantly to me. "I'll walk you and Fen home," he said, eyeing the carpet. I didn't dare look at the others or they might have noticed my sparkling eyes.

The conversation wasn't easy on the way to Fen's house. Danny walked between us. It was nice to feel protected in the dark. We stuck to safe subjects like teachers at school. Danny said that he liked Mrs Merle too, and

I thought how nice it was that we were already finding things we had in common.

We said goodbye to Fen at her house and I suddenly felt nervous to be on my own with Danny. I also felt excited. I wondered if he was going to be my first boyfriend. Danny was talking about his computer. He was crazy on computers. I wasn't interested in the slightest but I liked listening to the sound of his voice and it gave me the chance to daydream.

I was imagining going to the cinema with him. I knew I'd be the envy of a lot of other girls because he was good-looking and tall, and a very good runner. He'd even run for the county. I imagined myself amongst the on-lookers at an athletics meeting, watching Danny sprinting towards the finishing tape... Yes! He's *won*!

The crowd burst into cheers as they clapped their hands sore, but Danny only had eyes for me as he fought his way through eager autograph hunters to be at my side. His eyes never left my face as he got nearer and nearer and...

"We're here, aren't we?" his voice came crashing into my imaginings.

"Yes … we are…" I said, blushing furiously and thinking thank goodness it's dark, and thank triple goodness he can't mind-read.

The door opened. "Hello," said Mum, looking surprised but pleased to see Danny. I noted this as something good for the future. "Come in, Danny. It was so kind of you to walk Leah home."

"No problem, Mrs Bryan. OK, I'll just come in for a minute."

That proved it. He wanted a bit longer in my company.

"Hi, Dan." Kim had come into the room.

"Hi, Kim…"

And at that moment, the bottom fell out of my world. All she did was flick her hair back and flash him one of her mantrap smiles, but I'll never ever forget the look of admiration in Danny's eyes. Of course. It was all so blindingly obvious now I was confronted with it. It wasn't *me* who Danny fancied. I was just the means to the end. It was Kim he was after.

I mumbled something about finishing off my homework and slipped out.

Chapter 4

The next morning when I woke up, the horrible memory hit me in the pit of my stomach then gradually moved up to my brain. My brain played back the previous evening on fast forward, then switched off completely, leaving me lying there like a zombie – a very miserable, depressed zombie. To make matters worse I remembered that this was the dreaded Music Festival Day. "Please let me forget about Danny Johnston," I said over and over again to the four walls of my room, then I got dressed as fast as I could, and started practising vigorously.

I could feel my heartbeat speeding up as we

walked into the centre where the Festival took place. The building had a certain smell about it. I would always associate that smell with feeling nervous. Mum was in a very sparkling, happy mood. She loved music festivals, especially when I did well and she could be proud of me. I generally managed to get a certificate for coming second or third even if I didn't win, but this time I wasn't so sure.

"There they are!" cried Mum excitedly. "Jocelyn, we're over here!" she called, as she waded through the busy foyer packed with teachers, parents and nervous candidates all clutching music cases and instruments.

I began to get irritated before we even got close to them. Why did we have to have such pretentious friends? Jocelyn and Mum kissed each other – well they *almost* kissed each other, but they were both aware of the other one's glossy lipstick, so they kissed the air somewhere near each other's cheeks. David and Dad shook hands heartily, then the men kissed the women and I waited in the background feeling about eight years old.

Kim had gone shopping with her friends. It was the first year she'd managed to get away with missing the great family event, but I certainly missed her.

"Where's Oliver?" I asked after Jocelyn and David had both come out with the required clichés about how I'd grown and how nice my hair looked. It actually looked awful because Mum had insisted that I clip it back in a half pony-tail, so that it flowed about my shoulders, instead of being in the bun I always preferred. She even wanted me to put a ribbon round the pony-tail but I drew the line at that.

"He's somewhere about," said Jocelyn looking round. "Oh, there he is," she added. But there was something wrong. Where was the usual fond gaze and gooey voice that she kept specially for her precious son? Had Oliver done something awful which had turned his mum against him? I wondered, looking over to where her hand had vaguely waved. My first thought was, no, that can't be Oliver. But I was wrong because the next minute he was strolling over to us – and I mean strolling!

In just one year he was utterly transformed. Gone was that rather pathetic, goody-goody, industrious boy with glasses, spots and short neat hair. In his place stood a tall, floppy-haired, well-built boy, with not a single zit, no glasses anywhere in sight, and – get this – an earring. I just stared in total admiration and realized that my fast-beating heart was actually now racing for entirely different reasons.

Luce is always going on about different boys and how wonderful they are, but the rest of us think she's utterly mad, although we always enjoy listening to her because it's so entertaining. She falls in love at least twice a week and often with totally unsuitable people, like Mr Blundell – or Billabong as we call him – the tec teacher.

And now here was I, Leah Bryan, getting all starry-eyed about someone I had always thought of as utterly stupid. Uh-oh! Warning bells sounded in my head. I mustn't make the same mistake again. I didn't want any more mega disappointments. I came back to earth with a start because I could hear Mum sounding dramatic and not very happy.

"Oh, look," she was saying, "look what it says, Stu…" (This to my dad.) "Look, Leah…"

I dragged my eyes to the large blackboard propped up on an easel in the centre of the foyer:

SINCERE APOLOGIES TO COMPETITORS IN CLASS 18 (THE UNDER 16s OPEN). OWING TO CIRCUMSTANCES BEYOND OUR CONTROL, THIS CLASS WILL NOW TAKE PLACE AT 1.15 INSTEAD OF THE ADVERTISED TIME OF 11.40.

"I don't want to be late for the café," I immediately said to Mum in alarm.

"It's not the café I'm thinking about. It's the whole day's plans ruined," Mum said dismissively.

"But the café is actually quite an important part of *my* day's plans," I said to Mum with some hostility, which was unnecessary because I was sure I wouldn't be late.

"I knew you shouldn't have committed yourself to working there on such an important day," Mum snapped.

"I committed myself to the café when I first said I'd do the job," I told her, raising my voice. "All I'm doing now is trying to stick to that commitment."

Dad decided to put his oar in at this point. Slipping an arm round my shoulders, he said to both me and Mum, "Let's get these other two classes out of the way shall we, then think what to do. It's the under fourteens set piece, then the under sixteens set piece, then we'll get something to eat. Hm?"

He was right, which was unusual for Dad, and just shows that in actual fact he's not half as vague as he makes out. We all hurried to the large hall and sat down quite near the back because there were no places further forward. Oliver sat next to me and asked me what I was playing. I suddenly felt tongue-tied and silly.

"Oh, it's just this sonatina," I said, handing him the music.

"Oh, yeah, this is good," he said. "I played this just before I gave up."

"You gave up?!" I practically screeched.

"Ssh," said Mum with a fierce frown. "They've started."

"Tell you later," he whispered, and then I sat back ready to listen to the same piece being played thirteen times. I was number thirteen – the last one to play. A great omen! I sank into my own daydreams as some lovely smell came wafting over from Oliver. Is it aftershave? I wondered. Surely he doesn't shave already. I tried to look at his face without turning my head, but my eyes wouldn't go far enough to the left and I didn't want him to see me looking.

Don't ask me how the first ten people played the sonatina. I really don't know. Normally I would have been on the edge of my seat listening to every note, comparing every interpretation with my own, feeling anxious when I heard someone play it more slowly or faster or more detached or whatever, wondering uneasily whether I should change my own interpretation. My teacher had told me over and over again never to change anything, even if my version came out sounding totally different from everyone else's.

But this time was different. Apart from Oliver's trainers, Oliver's socks, Oliver's intoxicating scent, Oliver's faded jeans with holes in the knees, Oliver's long strong fingers and Oliver's thick silver and black ring on the middle finger of his right hand, I was quite unaware of anything, until I felt something irritating and repetitive trying to push its way into my little rapturous world.

"Leah!" hissed Mum, and I realized she'd been tapping my knee for quite some time, trying to attract my attention. "For goodness' sake, concentrate. I don't know what's the matter with you. Look, there's Mrs Locket. Get Oliver to swop places with her."

Oliver heard what Mum said, and dutifully jumped up to let Mrs Locket, my piano teacher, sit down next to me. He then sat down himself two places to her left. Normally I would have been grateful to have my teacher at my side, but not now. Oh, no. Instead, I felt rather cross with her for removing the object of my daydreams.

Number eleven was actually the first person I listened to properly, and I thought he played the piece really well. Mrs Locket was pointing to my music, then turning her face to me and making all sorts of smiley eyes. This was her way of saying, "He didn't play that bit as well as you can," or, "Look at that. It clearly says 'F' (which means loud) in the music, and yet he's playing it softly." I began to focus my attention and feel the adrenalin flowing through my body. I stretched and rubbed my fingers, then tapped a few scales out on my legs to get warmed up.

Number twelve was better than number eleven and I began to panic slightly. I mean, I'd only listened to two entrants properly, and they both sounded pretty good to me. The standard must be much higher than usual this year, I thought. I sneaked a look at Mrs Locket's programme. She always wrote down beside the name of each competitor the mark that she thought the adjudicator would give them. It was out of a hundred. She'd given only three of the competitors a mark in the nineties: number eleven – 91, number twelve – 93, and number seven, who I hadn't even heard – 96!

"Number thirteen – Leah Bryan," called the organizer from the front as she scanned the audience. I stood up shakily and stepped over Mrs Locket's feet to get to the aisle. The man sitting next to Mrs Locket hadn't tucked his feet in quite so neatly and I tripped over one of them and fell forward rather awkwardly into Oliver, who had stood up to let me get out. His hands gripped my arms firmly to steady me, then he bent down to retrieve my music! I had spent the last five minutes getting myself into I'm-about-to-play-the-piano-in-front-of-an-audience mode, and now here I was, back into I–think–Oliver's–so–cool mode!

"Go and show 'em how it *should* be done!" he whispered, with a wink. I gave a shaky smile back, then walked down to the front and up on to the stage.

"Now concentrate," I told myself fiercely. "Do it well – for Oliver," I added, but I really just wanted to get it over with. I started to play and a lovely feeling of relief that at long last I'd actually started, came over me. I played the sonatina rather mechanically. All my dynamics (that means louds and softs) were right, and all my phrasing (that means musical sentences) was good. My tempo (that's the speed) was accurate, and I didn't have any wrong notes. But I wasn't playing from my heart. I was just playing to get it over. At the end I walked back to my place with my head down because I hate seeing people's reaction.

Oliver didn't say anything as I slipped past him. Mum and Mrs Locket, on the other hand, both patted my knees, then both leaned into me and, one in each ear, whispered, "That was very nice, Leah." I giggled because neither of them realized that the other one was whispering in my other ear at the same time, and also, it tickled!

Well, that was one hurdle over with. I just had to wait for the results. I had the feeling that a great tradition was about to come to an end, because it would be a miracle if I came in the top three.

The adjudicator stood on the stage smiling round at everyone over the top of her glasses. She was clutching a wad of comment sheets. There was always one for each competitor. What power she has, I thought. She's about to make someone very happy, and she's also about to ruin someone's day. Some adjudicators were really horrible and hard on the competitors. Last year's adjudicator was one of those. She told a nine-year-old girl that her playing was heavy and plodding with no musical feeling or expression at all. She didn't say one single nice thing about that girl's playing and afterwards I saw the girl crying.

Then I heard from Fen's younger sister, Rachel, who goes to the same Brownie pack as the girl, that she'd given up piano after that Music Festival because she thought she was useless.

"Well, we've heard a great many interpretations of the Clementi Sonatina in C, first movement," began the adjudicator. She paused and added, "A *great* many." Then she smiled round at everyone again, over the top of her glasses, which made several of the adults in the audience titter.

Oh, she's one of *those*, I thought flatly. I couldn't stand the type of adjudicator who gave you a thin layer of comment and a thick layer of wit, designed specially to go over the heads of the competitors, and entertain the adults. This woman stood very solidly and heavily on high heels that looked too fragile for her. She was what Luce would describe as a typical overweight, middle-aged woman, whose clothes were expensive enough to hide most of the damage. Luce could be very perceptive.

I sank back into my seat and folded my arms over my music which I clutched to my chest. I wasn't looking forward to the next ten minutes. Some adjudicators managed to tell you the marks and to give some quick helpful hints in about three minutes, but I knew this one was going to be drawn out.

"Sit up," Mum hissed at me. "You look as though you couldn't care less about the marks."

I slowly heaved myself up by about three centimetres and gave a big sigh for Mum's benefit. Mrs Locket stabbed her programme and thrust it under my nose. She wanted me to see what mark she'd predicted for me. It was ninety-four. So she thought I was going to come second.

The adjudicator was going into great detail about how she felt the piece should have been played. She kept clicking over to the piano and playing a couple of bars here and there, then deliberately playing it badly to imitate what she had heard from some of the entrants. It made me sick the way she was mocking us. It made me even more sick the way the adults were lapping up her little performance. Then quite suddenly she stopped the lecture and flashed through the results...

"Number one – a little heavy – 74. Number two – quite a nice interpretation but just a touch slow – 81. Number three – a few slips in the middle section, otherwise quite nice – 78. Number four – needs to be a little lighter – 75..." and so it went on ... and on...

Mrs Locket and Mum had their heads slightly tilted to one side and an expression of great concentration on their faces, so as not to miss a single mark on this fast conveyor belt of results. "Number seven – 96. This was a stunning performance, quite breathtaking. Well done, David Brompton!"

At this point Mrs Locket proudly showed me, then Oliver, then Mum and Dad, the mark she had written beside number seven on the programme. She was obviously so delighted with herself for this clever little prediction, that she then turned round and showed the people on the row behind, who tried to look impressed, but probably thought she was batty.

The audience broke into applause. I clapped half-heartedly, not because I felt any malice towards David Brompton, simply because I didn't particularly like the adjudicator. She rattled off the next few results which were all in the low eighties, and I felt my heart beating faster as she got to the last four. "Number eleven – 90. Another lovely performance, just a little too much *rubato*. Number twelve – also 90. Again just a little too much *rubato*. And number thirteen…"

I held my breath. "Quite nicely prepared, but I just felt that this candidate didn't pull out all the stops today – 89."

With that, the smiling, clicking, entertaining, power lady had one final smile round at her captivated audience who applauded her heartily, then she left the stage. Mum was patting my arm distractedly, as though she felt I needed comfort but she couldn't quite find the words to go with it, because she was secretly very disappointed that I'd only come fourth.

I glanced at Oliver. He wasn't in his seat, he was by the door. Correction, he was *out* of the door!

"I'm just going to get some fresh air, Mum…"

I didn't wait for an answer.

As I was just leaving the hall I realized that Mum was trying to tell me something, but there was so much noise I couldn't work out what it was. I just nodded because I was holding people up who were trying to get out. In the foyer I caught sight of Oliver looking at a plan of the centre.

"Hi," I said. "I don't think I'm golden girl of the moment right now." I grinned at him but he didn't even bother to look at me or anything.

"Are you planning a break-in or something?" I asked him, rather wittily I thought, with a quick nod of my head towards the map he was studying.

"I want to find a room with a piano," he

told me, rather coldly. I couldn't work out why I was getting this frosty treatment from Oliver of all people. After all, why should he care how well or badly I played. I didn't know why he'd even bothered to come to the Music Festival when he'd given up music. He probably thought it was pathetic and childish entering silly little music competitions.

"Come on," he said briskly, and he set off at a hare's pace down one of the corridors. I followed behind, rushing to keep up and feeling rather foolish. Then I'd suddenly had enough. I was fed up with people bossing me around.

"I'm going outside," I told his back in a neutral voice. That made him turn round and look at me.

"You said that with about as much expression as you put into that sonatina just then. In other words – none! What's the matter with you, Leah? You should have won that class. The adjudicator was quite right when she said you didn't pull out all the stops."

"Well, I didn't feel like it, that's all," I told him, sounding very childish no doubt, but not caring any longer. "What's it to you anyway?"

He ignored my question and asked one of his own. "Why didn't you feel like it?"

I could hardly tell him that I was so dumbstruck by his transformation that it totally threw me, could I? So I just bit my lip and rather pathetically said, "I don't know."

"Come on," he said, sounding a little kinder. I followed him into a room with a piano.

"Are we supposed to be in here?" I asked. "It's not one of the designated practice rooms."

"There'll be loads of people in there. Nobody'll think to come in here. Now play that piece again and give it your best shot this time." He sat down on a desk and waited. I couldn't get over this new dashingly confident Oliver. I put my music on the piano and tried a few bars but stopped abruptly.

"I can't," I said. "I just can't at the moment."

"Yes, you can. Just pretend I'm not here."

It was impossible to do that, but on the other hand, I desperately wanted to impress Oliver. It seemed I was totally wrong. He *didn't* think music was childish and stupid at all. I played it again and stopped at the same place although I knew it was much better.

"Yes, you see, I knew you could. Go on, play it all like that." It must have been his praise that lifted me, because I played it right through, and even to me, it sounded like someone else playing from the girl I'd been in that hall. When I'd finished Oliver punched a triumphant fist in the air and said, "Yessss!!! Ninety-eight!"

I burst out laughing, feeling ridiculously happy, and said, "Why did you give up music Oliver?"

"I dunno. I just wasn't interested any more – except in blues music. I teach myself now."

"Play me some blues – go on."

I then listened, completely rapt while Oliver played the most amazing blues I'd ever heard.

"That was brilliant," I said when he'd finished. "I wish I could play like that."

"I'll teach you how to do it. It's dead easy."

Fifteen minutes later I suddenly shot off the stool and into the air. "*Omigod!*" I squealed looking at my watch. "*I've missed it!*"

"It's only twelve o'clock..."

"Yes, I know but I was supposed to be playing in the under sixteens set piece," I told him, as I sank despondently back on to the stool.

"Omigod," he agreed.

"Mum and Dad will be going frantic – not to mention Mrs Locket..."

"Come on," Oliver said with a sigh, "we'd better go and face the music." He gave a brief little laugh at his pun and we made our way back to the hall.

Dad was standing in the middle of the foyer looking puzzled and anxious. His face lit up when he saw Oliver and me approaching. Dear old Dad. He tried to look cross, but there was no mistaking the relief on his face when he realized that nothing had happened to me.

"Wherever have you been?" he asked, sounding exasperated. "Your mother's going mad with worry."

"Sorry, Dad, we lost track of the time."

At this point Mum came crashing out of the hall with Jocelyn, David and Mrs Locket in her wake.

"You've ruined the whole thing, Leah! What *have* you been doing? I don't know what you can be thinking of. Mrs Locket's been sitting in there wasting her time. She came to hear *you* play, not nine other people. And you go off gallivanting with Oliver. Just because Oliver's acting irresponsibly by giving up all that good musical training, and wasting his time on silly modern stuff, doesn't mean *you've* got to follow suit."

"I'm sorry, Pat," Jocelyn interrupted Mum with a face like thunder, "it is certainly *not* silly modern stuff that Oliver plays. It takes a lot of talent to play blues music, and anyway it has absolutely nothing to do with Leah's missing her class. And I'll thank you to keep your opinion to yourself in the future!"

At that point both husbands put their arms round their wives' shoulders, and looked very embarrassed and tongue-tied.

I sized up the situation in about three seconds. This is the damage I had managed to do:

1) Make everybody frantic with worry.

2) Waste Mrs Locket's time.

3) Let myself down.

and 4) Cause an argument between Mum and Jocelyn –

and I mean a serious one, because Mum looked as though she was on the point of bursting into tears and Jocelyn was being led away by David to calm down.

"Stop! Don't go, please!" I said to Jocelyn. She stopped. Everyone stopped. I even had the attention of several casual onlookers, but I didn't care, I just wanted to undo some of the damage.

"Look, I'm very sorry, OK? It's all my fault. Oliver wanted me to prove that I could still play the piano after that not very stunning performance in there," I said, with an apologetic smile at Mrs Locket. "Mum didn't mean what she said about Oliver and blues, Jocelyn. She's just wound up because of me. So, please, everybody take this as my official apology for missing the class. I just forgot the time. I'm sorry."

There was the teeniest of silences, then to my great surprise I heard people clapping. Our little group looked round to see at least a dozen strangers standing round in a grinning circle, applauding my speech. Oliver cracked up laughing, then Dad and David joined in, and finally even Mum and Jocelyn were standing together and laughing away. I looked down to hide my embarrassment, then turned to Dad.

"I'm starving," I whispered.

"Me, too. Let's get a quick snack in the cafeteria before the one-fifteen class."

The world seemed a happier place than it had done for ages as we all trooped down to the cafeteria.

Chapter 5

At one-fifteen I sat on my own near the front of the hall. I didn't want the distraction of Oliver beside me this time. I studied the programme and saw that I was number four of seven competitors. This was the class where each competitor was allowed to play a piece of their own choice. Anyone of *any* age could enter this class. It was the most difficult of the day.

Glancing round I had already spotted Claire Sellars who was a genius and devoted her entire life to music. Then there was Gabi Vicelli who also played fantastically. Sitting all hunched over, on the end of my row was a boy called Daryl Taylor who rattled off great long Schubert pieces without any music. He somehow never quite won, but always came second. I didn't recognize the names of the other competitors, but it was bad enough knowing about these three because I was going to sound awful compared to them. There was no way I could even get up on the stage, my knees were knocking so much. The audience would laugh when they heard my stupid little Haydn sonata amongst all those really difficult whizz pieces. I began to feel sick.

A little bell was rung to tell the audience to be silent, and the first competitor's name was called – "Daryl Taylor, please." Daryl stood up, still hunched over. His chin was practically touching his chest. In this pose he shuffled along, then stodgily went up to the stage and plopped down on the stool like a sack of potatoes.

"Would each competitor kindly announce the name of their piece before playing, please," came the adjudicator's clipped official voice. Daryl stood up, raised his head a couple of centimetres and mumbled, "Schubert's Impromptu Opus 90," which nobody sitting any further back than the second row could possibly have heard. He then sat back down on the piano stool and underwent his usual amazing transformation.

You see, Daryl Taylor (the person) is one thing, but Daryl Taylor (the pianist) is quite another. He slowly puffed out his chest, raised his shoulders, lifted his head, then lifted it a little bit more, till you thought he was about to attempt a backflip off the stool or something. Next his arms rose up dramatically with long fingers hanging like elegant bananas from his wrists. Then just at the moment when his whole body looked as though it was about to rise from the stool, he suddenly lowered his head, threw himself and his agile fingers at the piano and made the most beautiful sound fill the hall. The audience actually gasped in amazement.

There was no way I could even think about playing my piece after this. I felt more sick than ever. My hands were trembling and my knees were knocking. The more Daryl played, the worse I felt, until finally the horrible realization hit me that I *was* actually going to be sick. If I left the hall in a hurry, everybody would look at me and think, What a rude girl, interrupting Daryl's lovely playing. On the other hand if I stayed and threw up, it would *really* interrupt Daryl's lovely playing!

There was only one thing for it — I got up and ran out with my hand over my mouth. I didn't look to right or left, yet it was obvious that every pair of eyes in that hall watched my exit. I bolted straight into the loos and nothing happened. I waited, but still nothing happened. Then I realized that although I felt absolutely awful, I wasn't going to be sick.

I walked slowly back to the foyer and peered through the little window that looked into the hall from the back. A great burst of applause met my ears, so Daryl had obviously just finished. I noticed Mum was beckoning me energetically from her seat half-way down the hall. I shook my head at her, giving her at the same time the benefit of my most sickly expression. She immediately said something to my father which made him, Mrs Locket, Oliver, Jocelyn and David all turn round. Mum then came hurrying out as the next competitor's name was called.

"Whatever is the matter now?" she asked, looking older by the minute.

"It's no good, I can't play, Mum. I feel really sick."

Clapping a hand to my forehead she stared into my face as though that would determine whether or not I was just sick or seriously sick. Then after a pause she said, "You can play just as well as Daryl Taylor, you know."

"No, I can't. I'm useless compared to him," I told Mum. "And have you looked at the programme? Have you seen who else is in it? Claire Sellars and Gabi Vicelli. I don't mind coming last, Mum, but I don't want to come last by a mile. Anyway I'm far younger than all the others. Why did Mrs Locket have to put me in for this class when I'm only thirteen? Why couldn't she wait till I'm fifteen?"

"She wouldn't have entered you if she didn't think you were good enough."

"Listen," I instructed Mum. We tilted our heads towards the door. Strains of the Chopin D flat major Nocturne came floating through. It was absolutely beautiful and much better than I could play in a million years. And this wasn't even Claire Sellars or Gabi Vicelli. It was some girl with a very thick wiry-looking pony-tail and a big pink jumper. "It's no good Mum, I've told you. I'll be sick if I even go up on the stage."

Loud applause made us both turn back towards the door. The audience loved Miss Wiry Hair. I wished I could actually *be* sick, then there'd be no argument. The hall door opened and Mrs Locket and Jocelyn emerged.

"Come on love, buck up," said Jocelyn as though I was a bull about to face the matador. I ignored her. She had no idea how I felt. Looking through the door I could see Gabi

Vicelli standing on the stage announcing her piece.

"I wouldn't have entered you for this class if I didn't think you could cope, dear," Mrs Locket was saying gravely.

"That's exactly what I've been telling her," Mum said with a there-you-are look on her face.

"I'm sure you're nearly as good as this girl," Jocelyn added.

I'd suddenly had enough of everybody making clever little contributions about some-thing they just didn't understand.

"You must need your ears testing if you think I can play as well as this," I snapped at Jocelyn.

"Well!" she exclaimed, and Mum had to apologize to her for the second time that day.

"Don't listen to her, Jocelyn. She's not her-self. She's in a dreadful state."

"I feel sick and I'm *not* playing," I told everyone firmly. Then, thinking that that sounded rather like a spoilt little girl talking, I added, "Please, don't make me play, Mum.

I'm not good enough…"

"But it's you next, dear," said Mrs Locket in her most soothing tones.

"You can't let everyone down, you know," added Jocelyn, as though it was any concern of hers at all. Then all three of them started twittering and panicking because once again the audience were clapping like mad. I glanced through the door to see Gabi Vicelli doing a very deep bow, then throwing her silky black hair back and giving another bow!

"Come on," said Mum, opening the door and trying her best to physically thrust me through it. I just stood there feeling worse than I'd ever felt in my life. I could see the audience all turning round and looking over their shoulders. The adjudicator had obviously announced that it was number four, and everybody was wondering where number four had got to.

The next thing I knew, Oliver came out, took my hand, pulled me in, marched me down the aisle with a hand firmly on my back, then whispered so that only I could hear him,

"I'll give you five pounds if you don't come in the top three…"

"What!" I whispered back.

"And there's no way I want to part with five pounds so I must feel pretty sure of myself."

I gave him a look which said, "Do I have to go through with it?"

"Go on, show 'em." Then he gave me a gentle shove, and with a huge sigh I walked up the steps to the stage. My knees were still shaking, but my voice was steady when I announced my piece. By the time I was seated at the piano I felt full of determination. If Oliver thought I could do it, then I *could* do it, because I somehow instinctively knew I could trust Oliver.

I'd played the piece so often that I knew it backwards, so I didn't need to concentrate on the notes at all. All I thought about was the expression. After a bit I forgot about the audience, and just played. It was better than I'd ever played before.

The sudden burst of applause that hit my ears as I played the last note, made me jump because I'd completely forgotten where I was. I stood up and did a small bow. (I hate bowing, but that's what you have to do, so I did.) Then I raised my eyes for the teeniest moment to the row where my family and friends were sitting. Oliver was clapping above his head, Dad was wiping a tear away – dear old Dad. The others were grinning broadly. I went back to my place and as I sat down the most wonderful feeling of relief and achievement swept over me. I didn't care what mark I got. I felt that I'd overcome a huge hurdle.

The other three contestants all played much harder pieces than my little sonata, but it didn't worry me any more. It didn't even bother me when Claire Sellars, who was the last competitor, played her piece so well that the adjudicator actually had to raise her hands to get the audience to stop clapping. I wished I was sitting next to Oliver and the others instead of down here on my own, but I didn't want to draw attention to myself by moving.

The adjudicator was on the stage and the audience sat absolutely still and straight waiting to hear the marks. It seemed odd to me that complete strangers could take such an interest in a competition like this. I could understand the family and friends of each competitor, but not the rest of the audience, and the hall was certainly packed.

"How very privileged we all are to have been able to hear these young people's superb performances today!" began the adjudicator, which instantly prompted another enthusiastic round of applause. At that point I must admit my heart did start to beat a little bit faster and my mouth began to get a little drier. Some of the magic of having played and got it over with had begun to fade, and in its place was that old familiar feeling of anxiety about what mark I would get. Why should I care? I asked myself crossly, but I knew the answer to that one. If I didn't do well, Mum and Dad would be disappointed, Mrs Locket would be disappointed, Oliver would be disappointed and I would be disappointed. On the other hand, I would be five pounds richer!

"...not a big enough contrast," the

adjudicator was saying. Who on earth was she talking about? I realized with a jolt that I'd been wrapped up in my own thoughts, wondering what to spend Oliver's fiver on, because I was sure to win it. There was no way I could come in the top three. But, all the same, it was a clever way of Oliver's to get me to play.

The adjudicator sat down at the piano and proceeded to imitate Daryl and then to demonstrate how she would have preferred the music to have sounded. This is a bit tough on poor old Daryl, I thought. If she's as critical as this about *his* playing, whatever is she going to say about *mine*? My nervousness increased.

I only half listened to what the adjudicator was saying, but I couldn't concentrate properly because I'd just had a brilliant idea. I would ask Oliver if he wanted to come to the café with me at four o'clock. He could see where I worked. He was sure to be very impressed. I began to imagine difficult situations turning up, and me dealing with them perfectly, and Oliver sitting there, gob-smacked at what a mature thirteen-year-old I was. I smiled at the thought of this and for a fleeting moment my eyes met the eyes of the adjudicator, and it's a good job they did, because I suddenly realized she was talking about me and my piece.

"…and although Leah's chosen piece was not as technically demanding as the others, her playing was totally accurate and beautifully expressive."

I was so happy and relieved that the adjudicator had said such kind things about me that once again I went off into a daydream about Oliver and the café, and I didn't really hear much about competitors numbers five and six – Peter Tomlins and Erica Dutton. But I *did* listen to what was said about Claire Sellars, and the adjudicator was as complimentary about Claire as she was about me, only she said an awful lot more about Claire.

"And now for the moment you've all been waiting for…"

I held my breath and clenched my fists.

"The marks are as follows … Daryl Taylor – eighty-eight, Sarah Keene – (that must be Pink Jumper) – ninety. Gabi Vicelli – ninety-two, Leah Bryan – ninety three…" Ninety-three! I nearly collapsed. I'd even beaten Gabi Vicelli! "…Peter Tomlins – eighty-nine, Erica Dutton – eighty-nine and Claire Sellars–" she paused and I thought I was going to burst if I held my breath any longer – "ninety-three!"

The audience burst into fresh applause and I let my breath out. What a moment! I could have danced around the hall singing at the top of my voice I was so ecstatic.

I turned round to see Oliver making his way forward to me. "You owe me a fiver," he said.

"You didn't say…"

"Only joking!"

We both laughed and trooped out with the excitedly chatting audience, meeting the others in the foyer. Mum practically pounced on me and assured me that *she* would have put me even ahead of Claire Sellars if *she'd* been adjudicating. Mrs Locket gave me a hug and said she'd never heard that piece played better in her life. Jocelyn said she thought I'd played charmingly. Oliver looked at her as though she was a bit of dirt and said, "What do you mean 'charmingly'? Get real, Mum, she played out of her skin!" The men nodded and grinned knowingly.

"Would you like to see where I work?" I asked Oliver later when we were all in the sitting room at home, and the grown-ups were round the table deep into some very boring conversation about politics. I was filing my nails, so that my question about the café would sound very casual and not at all eager.

"Yeah, OK," Oliver answered. Great, I thought happily, but I just went on filing my nails as though I really didn't mind one way or the other. Kim and Danny were sitting very close to each other on the settee. They'd been shopping together and were obviously getting on really well. Danny's arm was across the back of the settee with his hand resting on Kim's shoulder. She didn't seem to mind. She looked very relaxed. I was sure I'd be straight as a ramrod if I were her. I glanced at Oliver. He looked very young compared to Danny, but that didn't stop me thinking he was the best thing since prawn cocktail crisps.

"I've got a good idea," Kim suddenly said. "Let's all go to the café."

She turned to Oliver. "It's a really great little place, Oliver. Loads of young people go there, especially on Saturday afternoons." I caught Danny's eye at that moment but we both quickly looked away. Seeing him sitting on our sofa with my sister, I couldn't imagine him in that crowd of boys, especially not with the horrible Barker.

"Can I phone Tash?" Danny suddenly asked.

"Yes, of course," Kim answered.

The telephone was right next to the settee, so even though Kim was chatting away and so were the grown-ups, I could still hear every word Danny was saying. Little by little my happiness seeped away as it became clear to me that Danny was inviting Tash to make up a four with Oliver.

Obviously Danny wanted Kim all to himself, and as I would be working, Oliver might have felt a bit left out. I know there was no reason why Danny shouldn't invite Tash to the café, and of course I was very fond of Tash, but somehow I felt that Oliver was *my* special friend, and I know it sounds stupid and petty, but I didn't feel quite ready to share this new cool Oliver with any of my friends just yet.

It all seemed so unfair. I'd already suffered one disappointment, over Danny. How short-sighted I'd been about that. I blushed to think about it. But this time I'd found someone my own age, well only a bit older, and I didn't think I could bear another disappointment.

Don't be silly, I told myself. They're only going to be together in the café for a little while, then Oliver will be back with me for the winners' concert this evening. The memory of Oliver telling his mum that I'd played "out of my skin" came flooding back and made me realize I was just being silly, and worrying about nothing. No. I could trust Oliver. I'd already decided that earlier on that day.

Chapter 6

At four o'clock I walked into the kitchen of the café to find Fen taking off her apron. I started to put mine on.

"As one beautiful girl disappears, another one drops in," said Kevin, in affected poetic tones. "What a lucky guy I am."

"Yeah, yeah, yeah," said Fen, pretending to yawn. Then she must have noticed that I wasn't exactly my most relaxed. "Oh, dear, *you* look fed up, Leah. Didn't you do very well at the Festival?"

"Yes. I came level first in one of the classes," I told her happily. "*And* the other contestants were miles older than me. I couldn't believe it."

"That's brilliant, Leah, I'm sure you're going to be famous one day, you know."

"In that case I'll have your autograph straight away," Kevin chipped in, "then I'll sell it for loads of money when you're a household name."

"There's not much chance of *that* ever happening," I informed him.

As soon as Kevin had his back to us, Fen mysteriously beckoned me to the opposite corner of the kitchen. She put her hand to the side of her mouth so that no one could even lip-read what she was saying, not that there was anyone around to take any notice except Kevin, who was deep into his pizzas by then anyway...

"You know about my novel that I'm writing," she whispered. I nodded because I knew that Fen wanted to be a writer when she was older. "Well, I've smuggled a tape recorder into the café. It's on that ledge near the heater. There's a vase of flowers in front of it, so no one will spot it. I was recording for half an hour earlier on."

"Why?" I asked simply.

"To get ideas for my novel. Anyway, somehow I've got to smuggle it out again because I want to listen to it tomorrow at home. Do you think you can nip in and get it for me when Jan comes out, if I keep her talking in here?"

An idea was forming in my mind. "Fen," I asked, "why don't you leave it in there, and I'll do some more recording for you, then I'll drop it back to your place tomorrow."

"That's a good idea, but don't forget to take it when you go, will you?"

Jan walked in as Fen pressed something into my hand. It was a blank tape. I slipped it into my apron pocket and went over to say hello to Jan.

"Bye, Fen," we all called as she disappeared.

"How did the Festival go, Leah?" Jan asked. It's so nice the way she takes an interest in what we all do outside the café.

"I was in three classes. The first one was not bad, the second one was a disaster and the third one was brilliant!" I explained all about it as we stocked up the delivery of Cokes, lemonades and ginger beers into the huge cupboard. Jan clapped and said, "Bravo!" when I'd finished, just as though I'd played her the piece! Then it was back to work.

"Right, could you transfer a few of these into the fridge? We're getting a bit low."

The fridge was in the café and I nearly bumped into Mark on my way through.

"Hi, Leah, how did you get on?" he immediately asked. So for the third time I related my tale. As I was telling Mark, and he was looking at me with such interest, I thought how lucky I was to be working with these nice people. Mark's only seventeen. He had left school at the first possible opportunity, and what he wants to be more than anything in the world, is a judo expert. He teaches judo every evening at a big leisure centre a few miles from Cableden. I think he's the assistant teacher.

It took three journeys to stock up the fridge, and on the last journey I saw Oliver come in with Tash. Kim and Danny were just behind them. They were obviously sharing a huge joke because all four of them were laughing. I felt a stab of jealousy and it took quite an effort to smile and say hello.

I was about to go back in the kitchen when I remembered the conversation I'd had with Fen. Checking no one was watching, I slipped the blank tape into the tape recorder and pressed RECORD. Kim and the others had sat down at a table next door but one to the tape recorder. I thought there was quite a good chance of their voices carrying though, because there was no one sitting at the table between them and the tape recorder.

"You look guilty! What have you been up to?" Jan asked as I went back into the kitchen.

"Nothing," I said, wondering if Jan could read minds, and feeling the tell-tale blush spreading up from my neck.

"Well, don't do it again," Jan said jokingly and I managed a strange little gulp of laughter, then started unloading the dishwasher for all I was worth, while all the time worrying in case Jan or Mark discovered the tape recorder.

Having denied I'd done anything wrong, it would be all the worse if I got found out. Perhaps I should remove it straight away before any more damage was done. As an excuse to go back into the café I took a pile of serviettes through.

"Could you clear and reset that table, Leah?" said Jan, on the run. It was the one between Kim's and the tape recorder, which hadn't been cleared from the previous customers. I got a tray and concentrated hard, so as not to make the same mistake as last time.

Kim and the others were so deep in conversation they didn't even realize I was right next to them. I tried to tell myself that it didn't matter, but I couldn't help feeling fed up that it was Tash sitting next to Oliver and not me. They were discussing films and videos.

"*Taco*'s on at the Majestic," Danny was saying.

"*Taco?* That's a brilliant film," Oliver said.

"Why don't we go and see it?" Danny suggested brightly.

"Yeah, that would be great," Kim answered.

"We could go tonight," Danny went on excitedly.

"Can I come too?" Tash asked.

"Well…" her brother began doubtfully. Then his tone changed completely as though he'd just had the brilliant brainwave of the century. "Why don't we all four go?" he suggested, looking round the table.

I walked off with my carefully-loaded tray because I didn't want to listen any more. Once in the kitchen I slammed the tray down on to the work surface.

"Oh dear, oh dear," quipped the ever merry Kevin. "Temper, temper!"

"Oh, shut up," I snapped, and for once he did, so I must have looked even more furious and fed up than I felt.

The next few minutes were spent on the phone because someone rang up about a children's party. She wanted to reserve a table for twelve which meant blocking off a part of the café. Jan had already explained to us how to organize a children's party and what to say on the phone. I thought I was probably the first one of the six of us actually to organize one, so I felt quite proud of myself, taking down all the details, and then checking in the store cupboards what extras we would need to buy. At least my mind had a rest from Oliver.

"Leah Bryan!" said Jan, leaning over me as I wrote. My heart missed a beat and I stopped writing. She must have discovered the tape recorder. Why else would she use such a voice? I braced myself. "You have made a truly excellent job of those party arrangements. Well done!"

I let out my breath and grinned at her. "Could you butter those scones and sort out this order? We suddenly seem to have a café that's bursting with customers. It's a very straightforward order ... table seven."

We were hardly ever allowed to serve, so I felt honoured. I must do it well, particularly as Oliver might be watching. I glanced in his direction as I went in with my tray for table seven, but again they were deep in conversation and didn't notice me. Then, horror of horrors, I saw who was sitting at the table right next to the tape recorder – Barker and the same three friends from Thursday. They were trying to tease Danny about being with a girl, but Danny was managing to ignore them.

I served the food to the table seven customers faster than they've probably ever been served in their lives, because I was desperate to get back to the kitchen before Barker spotted me. I'd almost made it when one of the old ladies from table seven called me back.

"Young lady … excuse me."

I turned and went back to her table. Barker's horrible voice came ringing out over the café in a ridiculous over-posh imitation of the old lady's voice – "Young lady, excuse me…"

Fortunately neither of the old ladies seemed to have noticed. They were probably a bit hard of hearing. "We don't need the jam, dear. You see, I'm diabetic so I've brought my own special jam. I just wanted to check that you don't mind me using my own jam in your café, dear?"

"No, I'm sure that will be quite all right," I assured her.

"Oh, yes, quate o rate," came Barker's nauseating voice, imitating me even though I hadn't spoken at all poshly. This time several people heard him and I walked back to the kitchen to the accompaniment of titters all round. The most depressing thing of all was that I was sure Oliver's laugh was amongst them.

I suddenly felt angry. Very angry. "Right, big mouth Barker, I'm going to get you back," I vowed to myself. "I don't know how, but somehow I will. You just wait."

After that I spent ages in the kitchen. There was plenty to occupy me – mainly washing-up, but I didn't mind in the slightest. Nothing would induce me to go back into that café if the Barker mob was still there. I kept thinking about the tape recorder though, and wondering if side one of the tape had finished yet. It must have done by now. If Oliver and that lot were still in the café I really wanted to turn the tape over and record a bit more.

The next time Jan went through to the café from the kitchen, I took a quick peek and saw that both tables were still occupied. One look at Barker's face reminded me that I didn't want to be in the same room as him, but on the other hand I was sure I heard him say something about judo, and he was looking directly at Mark as he said it. This was worth taping.

I filled a jug with water and went into the café. As I poured water into the vase of flowers in front of the tape recorder, I discreetly turned the tape over. Nobody could possibly have seen me do it because I was blocking everyone's view. I decided to do some more watering while I was at it, so as not to appear at all suspicious to Jan. I went over to the window where all the plant pots were.

"At least there's no danger of anything breaking when you're watering plants," said one of the Barker bunch. If I'd been Andy, I would have marched right over to their table, held a tray over the head of the person who'd made that comment, and said, "Oh, I don't know about that. I'd say your head was at risk, personally!" But, of course, I wasn't Andy so I didn't dare.

"It's amazing how many little jobs there are to do when you're a waitress, isn't it?" Barker joined in as I knew he would. "It must be quate exHORsting." His posh voice made the others fall about laughing, of course. I didn't look over for Oliver's table's reaction. I just tried to stay calm as I continued the watering, but I suddenly realized that I was tipping up an empty jug and pouring absolutely nothing on to the plant.

"Thank goodness she's not serving us. I wouldn't fancy an empty glass, would you?" Barker was really in the swing of amusing his admiring friends by now. I, typically, was going red, so I had to hurry back to the kitchen.

A couple of minutes later, Mark gave me a

message from Kim to say that they were going back home, then going on to see a film. "Oh, and she says she hopes the winners' concert goes well," Mark added. I thanked him, then turned back to my washing-up where a couple of tears dripping into the bowl didn't show at all.

At six-thirty, when I knew Jan was occupied at the till, Mark was in the kitchen and Kevin had long since gone home, I started noisily sweeping up round table legs with a brush and dustpan. When I got to the table nearest the tape recorder, I simply reached out and gently unplugged it. As I was straightening up I realized I was looking at a pair of legs. Uh-oh!

I stood up and Mark (the owner of the legs) raised his eyebrows at me and nodded at the tape recorder. "Don't tell Jan," I mouthed at him, with a pleading expression. He just grinned in reply and went back to the kitchen. I heaved a big sigh of exasperation. How stupid of me to get caught at the last minute like that. I thought I ought to give

Mark some kind of explanation. I slipped the tape recorder into my canvas shoulder bag and returned to the kitchen with the brush and dustpan. Jan was still working at the till with a frown of concentration on her face. She didn't even glance up when I walked past her.

"Taped anything interesting?" Mark asked as I walked into the kitchen.

"Um, I don't know," I answered cautiously.

"Let's have a listen then."

"No, we can't play it now. What if Jan comes in?"

At that moment Jan did come in, or rather she came crashing through the door in a tearing hurry.

"It's nearly twenty to seven and I'm supposed to be going out at seven o'clock and I haven't changed or anything! Mark, could you be an absolute gem and lock up for me? I've brought the board in but it needs a wipe over. You know the routine, don't you?"

"Don't worry Jan, I'll be careful."

"Thanks Mark, you're a star. Thanks Leah, pet. Have a lovely rest of the weekend, both of you. See you next week... Oh, and play well in your concert tonight. I bet your family and friends are proud of you."

"Thanks, Jan. Have a good evening."

"Bye."

And she was gone.

My family and friends can't be all that proud of me, I thought crossly, or they'd be there at the concert to support me, wouldn't they, instead of going to see *Taco* at the Majestic. I suddenly wished I'd got Andy with me. I couldn't remember what she was doing this weekend, but it was too late to phone her now because I had to rush home and get changed for the Festival concert. But first I couldn't resist just having a very quick listen to the tape.

Mark and I grinned at each other like naughty little children who were about to peep inside the Christmas presents before Christmas day. We rewound the tape until it was roughly half-way, then pressed PLAY because we couldn't be bothered to go right back to the beginning. At first it just sounded like a lot of strange little clonks and bangs with little bursts of laughter.

"I don't think it's a good enough machine to pick up anything other than background noise," Mark said, already losing interest and heading for the front door to start locking up. He stopped abruptly, however, as Barker's voice came over loud and clear. "Look at him, he thinks he's so clever, but he's not, you know."

Mark and I softly drew up a couple of chairs and bent our heads closer to the tape recorder. "Fancy working as a waiter. I'm going to get a much better job than that."

"That's a horrible year-eleven boy called Barker, from our school," I whispered quickly to Mark.

"Is this his job, then?" came another voice – one of Barker's friends. "Hasn't he got a proper job?"

Laughter.

"Probably stretches him to his limit. He was never all that bright at school." (Barker's voice.)

"He looks fit though. I bet he was good at PE, wasn't he?" (A different voice.)

"Useless. I could beat him at anything you name."

There was a pause after this last comment of Barker's, then quite a few voices speaking together so it was impossible to hear what was being said, then Barker's voice again.

"Look at Danny boy, out with the waitress's sister. Doesn't he look smug!"

"Me? Smug?" came Danny's voice. "At least I've got the sense not to boast that I can beat Mark Tillsbury at anything you name. I'd like to see you beat him at judo."

Barker's voice when he answered sounded as cocky as ever. "Course I could. Judo's for kids. You don't need years of training to chuck someone over your shoulder. You just need a few muscles. You need to work out at the gym like I do."

We couldn't decipher the talking that followed because of the amount of background noise. Mark pressed the STOP button, then sat staring at the tape recorder looking furious.

"That Barker needs sorting out, you know. I was at school with him. He's a year younger than me, and for quite a time he used to idolize me. Always following me about everywhere, he was, because I was the captain of the first XI football team and I won lots of gymnastics awards. Barker never quite made the first team and wasn't all that good at gymnastics either." Mark sighed and his angry expression softened.

"Oh, well," he said, "there's no point in taking these things to heart. If Barker wants to mouth off like that, that's his problem."

I thought how sensible and mature Mark was. He was worth twenty of Gary Barker. We got our things together, locked up, double-checked, then went out of the kitchen and locked that door too.

"I'd better run," I said to Mark, "or I'll be late."

"Hope it goes well," Mark called. "See you next week."

I ran all the way home with the tape recorder in my shoulder bag, banging against my hip. I was looking forward to hearing the rest of the tape, but it would have to wait till the next day.

At eight o'clock I sat down in the front row of the big hall and started nervously kneading my fingers to warm them up. The winners of all the different classes which had taken place during the day were also sitting in the front row waiting their turn, like me, to perform their piece. Claire Sellars was sitting about as far away from me as it was possible to sit. I didn't think she liked sharing first position with a little thirteen-year-old. She never once looked in my direction.

Mum, Dad, Jocelyn and David were sitting in about the fifth row, chatting happily. I turned round and Mum gave me a little wave, lifting her shoulders and smiling at the same time. She was in such a good mood. I wasn't. I couldn't help thinking about Oliver and Tash with Kim and Danny all sitting in a cinema watching a film together. The more I thought about it, the more depressed I became. I had been so sure Oliver liked my company. I knew a concert wasn't half as interesting as a film, especially a film like *Taco*, but it would be a long time till I saw Oliver again and I felt very hurt that he'd chosen to spend the evening with my sister, her boyfriend and my friend, instead of with me. I didn't know how I was going to play my piece properly. It's impossible to play well if you're not feeling like it.

The audience lights went out, leaving only the lights over the stage, which gave the hall a real concert atmosphere. A hush fell over the audience and the first player, who was only about seven, went up to the stage. There was no announcing this evening because all the names of the pieces were written on the programme.

After about half an hour my spirits were still very low, and the feeling of hurt hadn't left me. At last it was my turn. My teacher once told me it was good to feel nervous because that was the adrenalin pumping round your body, and it gave your playing an extra bit of zip. Oh, dear, I'm afraid my playing is going to be completely zipless, I thought flatly, as I put my music on the stand. Then somebody coughed in the audience.

I recognized that cough. I turned and looked out into the dark sea of faces. It only took a few seconds for my eyes to get accustomed to the darkness, then my heart leapt as I saw Kim smiling at me from quite near the back. Beside her on one side was Andy and Andy's mum, who must have driven them here. Then my spirits positively soared as I saw who was sitting on the other side of Kim. Not Danny, not Tash, but Oliver! So they'd come after all! The three faces I wanted to see most of all were all smiling up at me from the back. I could have cried with happiness.

Of course, the mere sight of Oliver sent the adrenalin pumping round my body. So when I sat down on that stool, I knew I was going to do it again. And I did! I played out of my skin! You should have heard the audience. They clapped and clapped long after I'd sat back in my seat in the front row. It was magic.

After that it was the interval. Andy came rushing up to me, flung her arms round me and said, "I just know you're going to be a big star one day, Leah, you were so fantastic. I'm really proud to be your best friend." I hugged her back happily as Kim came rushing over.

"Wasn't the film on or something?" I asked, trying to sound very matter of fact and not all that interested.

"Oh, Leah," she said, "I couldn't desert you. Danny was disappointed, but Tash said, 'Don't be silly, Danny, *Taco*'ll still be on next week and the week after, but this is an important evening for Leah and naturally Kim wants to be with her.'"

"But Mark said you were going to the film."

"No, it wasn't until after we'd left the café that I changed my mind."

So where does Oliver fit into all this? I wondered. He must have been dragged along by Kim, I suppose. Yes, of course. He could hardly stay with Tash and Danny when my family and all the rest of his family were here at the festival, could he?

I met up with Oliver in the refreshments room. He handed me a Coke and a bag of crisps as soon as I walked in. "You did it again," he said, with a grin. "The audience absolutely loved it."

"They haven't heard Claire Sellars yet, have they?"

"No competition," joked Oliver.

Then Dad came and put his arm round me. "Clever girl," he said, squeezing my shoulder. "I was proud of you in there." Dear old Dad.

The rest of the evening was great. I watched the second half of the concert with Oliver, Andy and Kim, then we went to a Pizza Hut where I realized how starving I was. I managed to quickly tell Andy about the tape recording, without the others hearing, and we arranged for her to come round to my place the next day to listen to it. I said I'd ring Fen too.

At the end of the concert, Andy, Oliver, Kim and I went back with Mrs Sorrell,

Andy's mum. She dropped us three off at my place then went on home with Andy.

"Thanks for coming to support me," I said as I got out of the car.

"Eet was nurthing but a pleasure," Mrs Sorrell informed me in her strong French accent.

"I wanted it to be a surprise," Andy said. "I phoned when you were out at the café – just to check you'd be playing."

Good old Andy! What a great best friend she really is.

Then it was time to say goodbye to Oliver. This was the moment I'd been dreading. It was cold and dark. The grown-ups were standing shivering by David and Jocelyn's car. Kim had already said her goodbyes and gone in. Oliver and I were a little distance from the adults. Personally I felt awkward and sad. I didn't know how Oliver was feeling. It was impossible to tell.

"Probably be quite a while before we get together again," he said.

"Yes, probably," I answered.

"Let's keep in touch ... shall we...?" he stammered. "I mean ... we could phone ... couldn't we?"

So, Oliver *did* feel awkward, too. That somehow made it better.

"Yes, we'll phone," I said.

"Come on, Oliver, we're ready to go," called Jocelyn.

"Bye then, Leah. See you sometime."

"Yeah, bye Oliver."

And then I went to heaven and back because Oliver kissed me. It was the fastest kiss in the history of mankind, but I didn't care. It was from Oliver, that was all that mattered. I could still feel it on my cheek long after the car's tail-lights had disappeared.

Chapter 7

Waking up on Sunday morning was so much better than waking up on Saturday morning had been. The memory of Oliver's kiss was the first thing that hit me which made me really happy. But the happiness was tinged with sadness because I wouldn't be seeing him for ages and ages. He did say he'd phone though. Correction, we both said we'd phone, but I thought I'd wait for him to phone first because I didn't want to appear too keen.

In fact, the more I thought about it, the more I realized that Oliver hadn't really shown very much keenness at all, apart from the kiss, and perhaps he always kissed girls when he knew them quite well. I mean, he hadn't been all that desperate to go to the Festival concert, had he? He would have been quite happy to go and see *Taco* with the others. It was Kim and Tash who felt sorry for me, not Oliver. He didn't feel anything.

Oh, dear. Here I was again, getting myself worked up and worried for no real reason. If I only knew for sure what was inside Oliver's head. The last thing I wanted was to be under the illusion that he really liked me if he didn't. The "Danny" episode was still a painful memory.

Later in the morning Fen, Andy and I sprawled on the floor in my bedroom and listened to the tape. Fen said she would listen some other time to the recording she'd done in the first part of Saturday afternoon, so we just listened to the tape I had done.

"You mean you taped Tash?" Fen asked, sounding a bit put out on behalf of her best friend.

"No, I just left the tape on like you did. It

wasn't to record anything or anyone in particular." That wasn't strictly true, but I didn't want to confess to my feelings about Oliver – not yet anyway.

"I think we should have a rule that if any of us is in the café, the person working isn't allowed to record."

"Good idea," Andy and I agreed.

"Listen to the bit about Mark," I said, rewinding the tape to try and find the place. "You see Barker was in the café…"

"Ugh! He's that revolting bully from year eleven who thinks he's Mr Cool, isn't he?"

"Yes, and yesterday was the second time this week that he and his stupid friends have been in the café. The first time was Thursday and he was making fun of me and calling out nasty comments."

"You should have told Jan," Fen said.

"I thought of that, but then I worried that Jan might chuck them out. Well, it wouldn't take Barker too long to put two and two together and realize who was the tell-tale. Then I'd really be for it! … Oh no! I've probably rewound too far now."

"Never mind, let's listen from the beginning."

So we did and it was very disappointing – that is until a familiar cocky voice filled the air.

"Do you think she will have noticed yet?"

"That's Duncan Peters, one of Barker's crew," I explained to the others.

"Who cares if she has?" said Barker. "There's no way she'll ever find out who nicked it."

"What if someone saw you take it out of her pocket?" (Duncan again, sounding rather worried.)

"You'll be in trouble if anyone saw me, because you were supposed to be keeping watch."

"Yeah, but it wasn't exactly a piece of cake with half the school milling about in the corridors."

Barker laughed then. "All the best pick-pockets work in crowds, you know."

"Stupid place to keep a ten-pound note

anyway – in your pocket," said another voice that I didn't recognize.

Fen, Andy and I exchanged open-mouthed looks, but didn't make a murmur for fear of missing the next bit of conversation.

"Yeah, it's just asking for it to be nicked, isn't it?"

"And she's supposed to be brainy, an' all!"

There was more laughter after that, and more conversation too, but nothing to interest us. We switched off the tape, and were all too shocked by what we'd heard to speak for a moment.

"So it was *Barker* who stole Jaimini's ten-pound note," breathed Andy, finally.

"Yes, and we've got the proof right here," Fen said. "There's no way he can deny it; he'll just have to pay it back."

It all sounded so obvious, so why was I worrying? "What's up, Leah?" Andy asked. "You've got that look on your face again."

"It's just that if we play the tape to Barker he'll be furious, won't he? He'd tell Jan for a start, and she'd go spare!"

Andy and Fen were frowning in concentration. "Leah's right," Fen said after a moment, "but why don't we just confront him with the facts? Just say we overheard him talking, and if he doesn't pay it back to Jaimini we'll tell Ms Chambers."

There was another pause for thought, then it was Fen who voiced her doubts. "Barker's going to be thrilled that we dobbed on him, isn't he?" she commented ironically.

"Hang on a sec," I said slowly. They looked at me hopefully. "I've got an idea."

"What?" they demanded in unison.

"Well, listen to this."

So I played them the bit about Mark. I also explained that Mark and I had already listened to it in the kitchen of the café. When Andy and Fen heard the tape they were really angry. "I bet Mark's absolutely fuming, isn't he?" Andy said.

"Well, he was at first, but then he just seemed to shrug it off. I really admired him. If it had been me I wouldn't have been able to forget it for ages."

"But what has this got to do with getting Jaimes' money back?" Andy wanted to know. So I told them my plan and they both thought it was a great idea as long as Mark agreed to play his part.

"Is there anything interesting on the other side of the tape?" asked Fen.

We played it through and after several minutes of loud noises which made it impossible to hear any conversation I suddenly heard Oliver's voice, but I couldn't make out what he was saying.

"Who's that?" Fen asked.

"It's Leah's friend, Oliver," Andy told her. "He's really nice. He went to the café with Kim and Danny and Tash so he could see where Leah worked."

We strained to listen but although we could clearly hear who was talking, we couldn't tell what they were saying. Then out of the blur came one clear word – *Taco*. "Oh yes, they were talking about films," I explained.

Another indistinct bit followed, then just when we were about to press the STOP button, Oliver's voice came over, just clearly enough for me to be sure I'd heard correctly. "Count me out, I want to go and hear Leah play," he said.

My happiness was complete. There was nothing left for me to worry or wonder about. Oliver hadn't wanted to go and see *Taco* as much as he wanted to go and see me play at the concert.

"He's really fond of you, isn't he, Leah?" Andy said sincerely.

I didn't answer. I just hugged my knees and my happiness to me.

On Sunday afternoon, we all met at Tash's house again to have another run-through of the recorder piece. This time the whole Johnston family was out, so we didn't get any interruptions from Peta, to everybody's disappointment. We worked very hard and got so good at the piece that by the end of the practice we knew it perfectly off by heart.

"Wouldn't it be great if we were allowed to play it in the school concert?" Luce said, looking rapturous.

"That's what I hoped right from the start," I explained, "for Miss Farrant's sake, really."

"Leah, you're far too nice and forgiving," Andy said warmly.

Monday morning, therefore, found us all prepared, but extremely jittery at the thought of everybody listening, particularly Miss Farrant. We had played it once through to Mrs Merle and she said it was "quite beautiful" and that Miss Farrant "couldn't fail to like it". This encouraged us a bit, but didn't stop the jitters!

When the hymn, the prayer and the announcements were over, Mrs Merle stood up and said, "A group of year-eight girls are now going to play you a recorder piece, written by Leah Bryan especially for her friends." She smiled at me and I led the way to the front. In a way I wished we'd had music to follow because as we were playing off by heart, I'd no idea where to look. At first I fixed my eyes on the clock at the back of the hall, but then I allowed my gaze to quickly scan the assembly of people, finishing on Miss Farrant. She was sitting at the piano, staring at the floor almost as though she was determined not to take any interest on any account.

We got through the whole piece without any mistakes, and I think everybody liked it because there was no shuffling or coughing. When we'd played the very last note, loud clapping broke out and we returned quietly to our places. As we passed Mrs Merle, she gave us a quick thumbs-up sign.

Ms Chambers, the Head, thanked us, and I glanced nervously at Miss Farrant to see her reaction. She was still looking at the floor. In fact I began to wonder whether she'd raised her head at all during our piece. Never mind. I had extra music practice for the concert at lunchtime, so she would probably mention our piece then, and hopefully she would suggest that we played it in the concert. I didn't really mind, I just hoped that it had impressed her enough to let Fen off any further punishment, and to forgive us for taking the recorders.

We were about to file out of assembly when Miss Farrant suddenly said, "Excuse me Ms Chambers, I have an announcement. I should like to see Fenella Brooks in my room at morning break."

So she hadn't forgotten. Poor Fen.

At the beginning of morning break, the six of us met in Fen's and Tash's tutor-group room, and decided that we'd all go and see Miss Farrant together. It wouldn't be fair to let Fen face the music alone. After all, we were all involved. Jaimini was determined that she would also do whatever punishment Fen had to do.

"We've got something to tell you afterwards, Jaimini," Fen whispered. "Something very interesting about your ten-pound note."

"Tell me now, go on," Jaimini begged, but we hadn't time.

Miss Farrant was in a brisk, no nonsense mood. "Right," she said, "I want to know precisely why you, Fenella, left detention early on Friday on the pretext of going to the lavatory, and did *not* return. And I want the truth!"

Jaimini and Fen looked at each other, then Jaimini took a deep breath and began the explanation. She and Fen took turns explaining about the café and our work rota, and also about the missing ten-pound note. Throughout all this Miss Farrant looked from one to the other of them, with no expression at all on her face. It was quite scary to watch because you had absolutely no idea whether she was going to break out in a fiery temper and announce gross punishments, or break into a smile (fat chance of that!) and thank us very much for an excellent explanation.

She did neither of these. She just looked very tired all of a sudden and said, "Wouldn't it have been an awful lot easier simply to have told me on Friday?"

I saw Fen get ready to defend herself, then change her mind. I didn't blame her. After all, she could hardly say, "How *could* we explain when you were in such a stinking bad mood? You might have decided to lock us in for the entire weekend or something."

"Concert practice at lunchtime, Leah, and don't forget," were her last words as we trooped out.

"She never even mentioned our recorder piece, did she, the nasty old ferret," Luce commented grumpily.

"Never mind, at least we got out of another detention," Jaimini said, sounding relieved. "Now, what have you got to tell me? I've been dying to know."

So we explained about Fen's tape recording and all about Barker and his friends and what they'd said. Luce, Jaimini and Tash reacted exactly as the rest of us had done when we first heard the tape.

"That proves it," said Luce hotly, "we can demand that he pays Jaimes back."

There was a brief pause, during which I'm sure everybody must have been doing a mental run-through of us six marching into year-eleven territory and "demanding" Jaimini's tenner.

"I don't think that was one of your better ideas, Luce," said Tash thoughtfully, which made the rest of us laugh because she said it in such a matter of fact way. Luce was not amused.

"So, what do you lot suggest, then?"

"Leah's got this great idea," Andy answered, leaning forward and speaking softly. We then all got into a huddle and I explained my idea.

It was Luce's turn at the café that day, but we all went along with her and as she disappeared into the kitchen through the back door, we went in through the front entrance and sat at a table for six.

"What kind of mood was Ferret-features in at lunchtime, Leah?" asked Andy.

"Very bad," I answered. "She spent the entire practice either shouting or tapping her baton on the music stand, or worse still, staring at us with those nasty, piggy eyes."

"I don't know why you put up with her, Leah," Tash said, which was quite strong for Tash.

"Yeah, why don't you leave her to stew?" Andy asked vehemently.

I shrugged my shoulders. "I don't know."

"You're crazy to put up with her stroppiness all the time. I'm surprised at the others as well, if there are any left."

"There aren't many, it's just the keen musicians, really."

"Well, *we* put up with her during choir practice, don't we?" Fen pointed out.

"That's only once a week," Jaimes commented.

"Well, I've had enough of it. Even once a week is too much," Andy said, and the others agreed.

"You must be mad, Leah," Tash persisted, "putting up with her several times a week."

"I know I'm mad," I answered, because I'd had enough of that conversation, and the truth was I didn't really know why I put up with it. I just couldn't quite break away for some reason.

"You're too nice, that's always been your problem," summarized Andy, who must have seen my discomfort. I smiled at her for saying such a kind thing, then quickly changed the subject.

"Anyway, where's Mark?"

"What can I get you girls?" came Becky's cheerful voice.

"Oh, isn't Mark here?" Fen asked, sounding disappointed.

"Terribly sorry I'm not Mark. I'll do my very best to take your order just as well as *he* would, I'm sure," Becky began, pretending to be upset.

"No, I didn't mean it like that," laughed Fen. "We just wanted to talk to Mark, that's all."

"Well, you'll have to wait twenty-four hours for that pleasure. Now what do you want to drink?"

We almost decided not to order anything because it seemed such a waste of money, especially for Jaimini, who was desperately trying to scrape ten pounds together to pay back Mrs Merle.

"It won't be long till we get Barker to pay it back, Jaimes," Andy said with feeling. I think of all of us, Andy loathed Barker the most. In the end I'd told her confidentially about the time he was mocking me over my badly-loaded tray, and she'd said she'd like to scratch his eyes out.

When we'd finished our Cokes and were about to go, in walked guess who? Yes, Barker. As usual, he'd got his little band of disciples with him.

"He couldn't manage without them, could he?" Andy whispered. I could already see her hackles rising. She really did hate him. "Why can't they just walk normally and sit down like everyone else?" she went on vehemently. "They have to drag their feet and swing their bags and make a load of noise scraping their chairs back, don't they?"

"Calm down, Andy," I said, feeling anxious in case Andy got so wound up that she said something which would spoil the surprise we had in store for Barker.

"Oh, look who it is – Brains and the drains," Barker commented loudly on seeing us across the café. His four friends laughed, and Andy, looking furious, pushed her seat back to stand up. I was on one side of her and

Tash on the other, and we both instinctively grabbed one of her arms each and held on, so she couldn't get up.

"I'm not sitting here and putting up with his big mouth," Andy said, through gritted teeth.

"I don't blame you." Fen added her support to Andy's. "Come on, girls, let's stand up to him."

The rest of us looked at each other with worried expressions. "We can't, it'll spoil it," Tash said. "Look, we've only got one more day to wait, then we can tell Mark the plan and he'll sort Barker out a thousand times better than we could."

"But what's the harm in just telling him what a toe-rag we think he is," Fen insisted.

"In fact, what's to stop us telling him we know about the tenner? It won't make any difference to the plan, will it?" Andy added.

"We don't want to take unnecessary risks, do we?" I said.

"Come on, let's go," Tash suggested.

"That's the easiest and quickest way to avoid his nasty tongue."

So we paid Becky and asked her to say "bye" to Luce for us. "You can say it yourselves. Here she is," said Becky.

Sure enough, Luce had emerged from the kitchen and was heading towards the table next to Barker's, with a full tray.

"Oh, it's Miss Frizzy with the two left feet," Barker remarked, which raised guffaws of laughter from the rest of the table. I saw Jaimini's eyes narrow. She always defended Luce, especially if anyone made reference to the fact that Luce was rather accident prone. Luce herself didn't appear to notice the remark. Either that or she was putting on a brilliant act. We'd got to the door by this time and Luce was just about to serve the last lemonade which she was holding in her left hand. The tray was on her other hand.

"Bye, Luce," called Jaimini, in scarcely more than a whisper, because Jan had always stressed that we must never call out across the café.

"Going already?" said Luce, looking at her watch. Of course, to look at her watch she had to turn her wrist over, which meant that the lemonade she was holding tipped out of the glass. She was standing right behind Barker's chair and we watched in shocked delight as the contents of the glass splashed on to his head, then down his face in little rivers.

Was it my imagination or did Luce take just a little longer than necessary to consult her watch? The whole thing seemed to happen in slow motion. It was absolutely riveting to watch and we weren't the only ones who were amused.

"I'm so sorry," Luce said, with a voice full of wonderfully-acted false sincerity, as she leaned over Barker and started wiping his face with a serviette. "Here, let me dry your face." By this time even more customers were looking and some of them were openly sniggering. Barker was furious. He grabbed the napkin off Luce and roughly wiped his face, calling her all sorts of names under his breath.

"I'm afraid I must have two left hands as

well as two left feet," Luce added wickedly, as Jan came rushing out of the kitchen with a towel. She didn't look very pleased at all.

"This clumsy girl has ruined my school uniform," Barker told Jan in loud, accusing tones. The rest of his table, who had been grinning and nudging each other a moment before, suddenly jumped to attention as their hero assumed his tough image again.

Luce gave us a very subtle wink and a smile as if to say, "What did you think of my performance?" For answer we gave her the thumbs up, then disappeared out of the door quickly. The last I saw of Luce she was wearing an expression of great concern and murmuring to Jan that she was sorry.

Becky closed the door after us, which gave her the chance to tell us discreetly that she'd heard what Barker had said to Luce and had alerted Jan to the brewing trouble. She assured us that Jan would not be cross with Luce, but was simply furious to be in the position of having to put up with Barker because he was a customer. And for better or for worse, in the café business, the customer is always right.

The next day we all met outside school as planned. Luce was the last to arrive and we welcomed her like a hero.

"You were brilliant, Luce," Jaimini told her warmly.

"Was it *really* an accident?" Fen wanted to know.

"No, it was cold-blooded revenge," Luce told us dramatically. "I just lost my temper when he called me Miss Frizzy. I didn't mind so much about the two left feet because it's true, but I thought my hair was getting straighter and not so thick, and I couldn't stand by without retaliating in some way."

"You really should be an actress, you know, Luce," Tash said with admiration.

"I intend to be," Luce answered with a determined look in her eye.

"Right, so let's all meet up after school and go and put the famous plan to Mark, yes?" Fen said.

"I'm on duty," said Andy.

"And I've got a practice after school," I said, that familiar sinking feeling coming over me.

"Never mind," said Andy, "as long as you're there to witness Barker handing over the ten pounds, that's all that matters."

"Thank goodness it's the school concert tonight," I said with feeling. "I can't wait to get it over with, then there'll be no more horrid rehearsals, no more boring practices..."

"No more ferrets sniffing you out when you forget the horrid rehearsals and the boring practices," Fen added.

"You know, I still can't forgive her for ignoring our wonderful recorder piece," Tash said.

"It wasn't wonderful. It was just average," I told them.

"No, it wasn't average," Andy argued. "I saw the reaction on everybody's faces — teachers and pupils alike, they thought it was brilliant, I could tell."

I smiled at Andy because she was being

kind, but I didn't believe her. I was obviously just getting too big for my own boots, expecting praise for a very ordinary piece. And the simple fact was, Miss Farrant obviously didn't think our recorder piece was good enough for her concert.

"See you after school, then," we all said, going off to our different tutor rooms.

Little did we know what lay in store for us before the end of school.

Chapter 8

In morning break I went dutifully off to the auditorium, leaving the rest of the girls sitting in Luce's tutor room, guzzling her cookery. It's great when Luce has double cookery first thing after assembly, because she's such an excellent cook and it means we get to eat what she's made at morning break – unless of course it's tuna pasta or something. On this occasion it was sausage rolls and we were all starving.

When I got to concert practice I found that Luce had stuffed a sausage roll in my violin case, but unfortunately it would have to wait till the end of the practice because Miss Farrant's mood was blacker than ever.

"Look! This concert is going to be very disappointing unless you all decide to put a bit of enthusiasm into your singing and playing. Now stop looking so bored and buck your ideas up a bit. Come on, let's get some life into it…" She paused and I saw the same look flit across her face that I'd seen the previous day when she'd seemed too tired to tell Fen off properly. As soon as it had come, the look disappeared and she was in full flow again.

"And where are the rest of the choir? I made it absolutely clear that I wanted everybody here this morning. Jaimini Riva and Natasha Johnston, Andy Sorrell, Lucy Edmunson and Fenella Brooks are all missing. I might have known it would be that lot. I suppose they've decided not to bother with choir because, despite the intervention of Mrs Merle, I'm not having their famous recorder piece in the concert. Is that it? Hmm? Leah?"

"No, Miss Farrant. They just didn't realize they were needed this morning. I'll go and get them."

"And be quick about it. The rest of you get in your places."

I ran as fast as I could down the corridor and into Luce's tutor room. Only Tash was there.

"Where are the others? They're supposed to be at the big rehearsal for the concert, in the auditorium. Miss Farrant's going berserk."

"They weren't feeling well. They've all gone to the loos."

"Oh, no…"

"Look, I'll go to the auditorium," Tash suggested, "and you go and get the others. I'll tell Miss Farrant that you're all on your way."

When I got to the loos I found Fen being sick, Jaimini clutching her stomach and looking very pale, Luce drinking water having just been sick, and Andy looking more worried than I thought I'd ever seen her. She did a huge sigh of relief when I walked in, and started gabbling urgently to me.

"Thank goodness you're here. I've been praying someone would come. They're all so ill, I didn't dare leave them. It must be a bug or something – a very violent one. Fen's been sick about ten times. She's got nothing else to throw up but her body keeps retching."

"It can't be a bug. It's too much of a co-incidence, all of them being sick at the same time. Oh, poor Fen."

"And poor me," said Luce, looking deathly pale.

Jaimini managed to whisper, "It must be what we ate."

Andy and I turned our heads in slow motion towards each other, wide-eyed with realization. "Sausage rolls!" we said at exactly the same moment.

"Did you eat one?" I asked Andy.

"I nibbled a tiny corner but thought it tasted funny, so I chucked it in the bin. I didn't tell Luce because I didn't want to insult her cooking. What about you? Did you eat yours?"

"No chance with Ferret-eyes watching. And Tash?"

"No, Tash said she wasn't hungry."

"That's it then. Whatever did you put in

those sausage rolls, Luce?" I tried to put the question as gently as I could because she was still looking green, though not half as bad as Fen, who had apparently eaten two and was still in a very bad state.

"I didn't put anything different from what I normally put in sausage rolls," said Luce in a most un-Luce-like whimper.

"Well, you must have done it by accident, then," Andy said.

"But Mum packed my cooking things. She'd never get it wrong," Luce carried on in her weak voice.

"Ssh!" Andy suddenly said.

"What?"

"Listen…" she whispered. "Someone's outside. I definitely heard someone snigger."

Andy has fantastic hearing and eyesight. She's also capable of moving at great speed without a sound. We've always said she should be a spy when she's older. Quick as a flash she moved through from the loos to the cloakroom, then went out into the corridor. A moment later she returned, eyes glinting, lips tight.

"That was Barker," she said. "He was just disappearing round the corner with the others, but it was definitely him."

"He must have put something in one of Luce's ingredients," I said.

"But when?" asked Luce in a small voice.

"During assembly," said Jaimini who was still clutching her stomach and rocking backwards and forwards.

"Poison!" said Luce, jumping up in a panic. "He's trying to kill us to get back at me for what I did in the café." Then she dropped back into her chair again at exactly the same moment as Fen collapsed on to the floor and lay there white and still.

"Oh, Fen," cried Andy and I, rushing over to her. She managed to mumble something, but we couldn't tell what. It was obvious there was something badly wrong with her.

"I'll go and get one of the teachers," Andy said. "Fen's really ill."

She ran out. Fen started to shiver violently and she didn't seem to be capable of opening her eyes for more than a moment at a time.

Jaimini was being sick by then so I got Luce to sit down on the floor beside Fen, then I gently moved Fen so her head was resting on Luce's lap. Next I grabbed a few coats and put them over her to keep her warm, then soaked a handful of paper towels in warm water and began to bathe her face. I didn't really know if this was what I was supposed to do but at least she looked a bit more comfortable.

It was Mrs Kenyon, the cookery teacher, and Mrs Merle who came back with Andy. "Well done, dear," Mrs Merle said to me as Mrs Kenyon felt Fen's forehead, then her wrist. Fen started to make a slight groaning noise and I saw a definite look of relief pass over the teachers' faces. Andy had obviously already explained about the sausage rolls because Mrs Merle started quizzing Luce on whether she might have possibly made a mistake with her ingredients.

"Mum measured everything out for me this morning," Luce assured her, in the same weak voice. "And Mum would never make a mistake like that."

"Have you told Mrs Merle about Barker?" I whispered to Andy. She shook her head quickly.

"What about Barker? Who's Barker?" said Mrs Merle and Mrs Kenyon at the same time.

"Gary Barker from year eleven," I said.

"What's he got to do with all this?"

"We think he might have…"

I stopped, because it was very risky, dobbing on Barker to the teachers. You never knew how he would react.

"Are you saying that Gary Barker may have added something to the ingredients that went into Luce's sausage rolls?"

Andy and I nodded reluctantly. The teachers looked at Fen and then at each other as the bell rang loudly, making us all jump. "Right, let's get Fen and the others to sick bay. We'll give Fen a chair carry, if you two can help Jaimini and Luce along the corridor."

Once in sick bay, the nurse tucked Fen up in bed with two hot water bottles and took her temperature. Luce and Jaimini sat down on a big sofa and Mrs Kenyon hurried off with pursed lips. We knew exactly where she would be going – to find Barker.

Fen's temperature was a hundred and two, even though she was still shivering. "This child has got food poisoning. There's no doubt at all about that," the nurse said to Mrs Merle. "Thankfully she's got it all out of her system, but the other two must have been poisoned too, and the sooner they can get rid of whatever it is, the better." As if on cue Jaimini staggered off to the loos to be sick. There was a knock at the door and Tash came in.

"What's happened?" she asked, rushing over to Fen.

"We think it must have been something in the sausage rolls because we three didn't eat any and we're OK," I told her.

Tash looked puzzled. "Mrs Kenyon's gone to get Barker," Andy continued. "I think I heard him sniggering outside the cloakrooms, and I definitely saw him disappearing round the corner when I went out to see. We reckon he may have doctored Luce's ingredients when she was in assembly."

Mrs Kenyon walked back in at that moment. We looked at her questioningly. "He's seeing the Head," she said for an answer. After a minute, during which we all looked gravely at Fen, who had fallen asleep, Mrs Merle said, "Why should Gary have done this? Who was he trying to get at? Has he got something against Lucy?"

Luce looked so pale and listless and incapable of answering any questions that Mrs Merle had been talking as though she wasn't even there. So it surprised us all when Luce sat up rigidly to attention and said, "It doesn't matter. It's not important." Then she turned to Andy, Tash and me, and garbled, "Don't tell her, please. You never know what he'll do next. I just want to be left alone." That much effort was enough for her and she sank back down into the soft sofa and yawned.

"These two girls need to go back home to bed while they're still awake," said the nurse. "We won't disturb Fenella, but they'll all three be much better when they've slept it off."

Mrs Merle looked baffled for a moment, then sort of sighed a thoughtful sigh and said, "Hmmmmm," as though she was working out a vitally important problem. Andy and I kept quiet for poor Luce's sake.

Tash knelt down beside Luce and said, "Don't worry, we won't say anything."

"I think you three had better go back to your lessons," said Mrs Kenyon, gently.

"Don't tell Mark the plan," Jaimini whispered to Andy.

"Why not?" Andy asked. "I thought it was all decided."

"Not now this has happened," Jaimini said.

There was a pause, then Tash said, "She won't say anything, don't worry."

The rest of the morning was double history but it may as well have been double Dutch for all I took in. As soon as the bell went, Andy, Tash and I rushed straight back to the medical office. Fen was still asleep and Luce and Jaimini had been sent home.

"Fen *will* be OK, won't she?" Tash asked the nurse shakily.

"Yes, she will, dear. Fortunately she got rid of the poison straight away, and now she's sleeping off the effects of the attack on her body." Tash decided to stay in the sick bay in case Fen woke up. Andy and I went for a walk outside together.

"Why didn't Luce want us to tell Mrs Merle what she'd done to Barker?" I asked Andy.

"I don't know. Perhaps she thought it would only stir up more trouble."

"Yes, but she knew that we'd already told Mrs Merle that we thought Barker might have tried to contaminate the sausage rolls."

"I suppose there's no proof of that, is there? I know I saw him outside the cloakroom, but he's sure to deny it, and anyway that still doesn't prove that he tampered with the ingredients, does it? In fact, we're on to a loser whichever way you look at it because even if Mrs Kenyon got the remaining sausage rolls analysed, and they were chock-a-block with arsenic, it *still* doesn't prove that it was Barker's fault. So I suppose Luce thought she'd better not say anything that might pile up the evidence against him."

"But why not? We *want* to prove him guilty, surely!"

"I'm not so sure now. You do and I do. But Tash is too worried about Fen to think about revenge, and Fen, Jaimini and Luce are scared stiff of what Barker might do if we get him into trouble by reporting everything he's done."

I looked at my watch. "I'd better go, Andy. At least this is the very last rehearsal." We were more or less outside the Head's office window at this point, but it came as quite a shock when the window was flung open and Ms Chambers called out to us. "Leah and Agnès, could you come to my office for a moment, please?"

"Oh, no," said Andy, "looks like we're going to have to incriminate him and risk whatever awful consequences he might decide to inflict on us all."

"Maybe not. Maybe this is our chance to try to get Barker off the hook. That'll make him grateful to us,. then he might leave us alone."

We stopped in our tracks and looked at each other. In one fleeting moment I watched Andy's expression go from sad and hopeless to dynamic and determined.

"Just listen to us," she said. "We must be mad! Here we are trying to save Barker's skin, and that nasty piece of work has taken ten pounds from one of our best friends, and poisoned three of our best friends, not to mention insulting you and Luce! He doesn't need our help. He needs nailing into the ground!"

"Yes, you're right," I said, as Andy's infectious determination rubbed off on me. "We won't let him get away with this. I'm sure Luce and the others will agree with us once they've got their strength back."

We ran to Ms Chambers' office, desperate to incriminate Barker in any way we could.

"Come in," said Ms Chambers. "Sit down, girls." She looked very grave indeed. Her voice was calm and slow, and full of a certain tone called I-am-the-Head-and-don't-you-forget-it.

"Now," she began. "I hear you have made some very serious allegations against Gary Barker. I want to point out to you that this isn't a matter we can take lightly. It is imperative that you keep your personal squabbles out of school. Teachers should only be involved in matters which directly affect school life, and in this case, the allegations you have made are so ridiculous that I think it would be better all round if you simply quietly withdrew them.

"I've spoken to Lucy Edmunson and she says she must have mistaken bicarbonate of soda or something else for flour when she got her ingredients together this morning…"

"But Luce didn't even…" Andy started to say. She wasn't allowed to continue, though.

"I trust you're not disputing what Lucy has actually told me herself, Agnès?"

Andy hung her head for a second, but being Andy, it shot up a moment later and she said, "Ms Chambers, have you spoken to Barker?"

"Yes, I have heard his side of the story…" She paused, then studied us hard as though trying to analyse our reaction with her next words. "He seems to think you've possibly got some kind of crush on him…"

Andy and I gasped and opened our mouths to protest, then shut them because Ms Chambers had not finished. "He mentioned some stunt that Lucy apparently carried out in the café, designed possibly to amuse her friends at his expense?"

Again her eyes were boring into us. It's always difficult to know what Ms Chambers is thinking and even more difficult to have a conversation with her because you always have the impression that she's controlling what you say and what you don't say. Creepy! We desperately needed to say something that would make Ms Chambers listen to us. It was Andy who came up with it.

"What about stealing ten pounds on the school premises?"

That got her attention. She looked most taken aback. She obviously didn't know what to say so she was playing for time.

"I'll discuss that with you in just a moment, Agnès, but first I want a quick word with you, Leah. Miss Farrant spoke to me about you a short while ago. She despairs of you lately. You're obviously a very musical girl and yet your commitment to the school's music leaves a great deal to be desired. You're continually late for practices – today being yet another example of that."

What a cheek! I thought, because it was Ms Chambers who had made me late by calling me in to see her.

"Sometimes you forget to turn up altogether," she went on, "and now I hear that you helped yourself to six school recorders when Miss Farrant expressly forbade you to do so. So I suggest you go along to Miss Farrant right now, and apologize *again* for your lateness at this, her final rehearsal for tonight's concert!"

"I did turn up this morning, but then I had to go and get the others, and they were ill, Ms Chambers."

"Well, I'm sure they haven't been ill for the last few weeks, have they?"

Andy gave me a look which said, "You're not going to let her get away with *that*, are you?" But I couldn't be bothered to retaliate. It was all so unfair. No matter what you said, it was always flung back in your face. What was the point? I mumbled "Sorry" and disappeared, leaving Andy to try and put our side of the story to the most difficult Head Teacher in the history of education.

What a bummer! I thought, as I dragged my feet along to the final dose of Ferret fun. Huh!

"Leah Bryan," she bawled at me as I walked into the auditorium.

Not again, I thought angrily. I braced myself, and took deep breaths through my nose, feeling like a dragon about to breathe fire.

"I am fed up with wasting my time rushing round this school trying to track you down. Go to your place this minute. You are getting just a bit too big for your boots if you think you can come breezing in here twenty minutes late, young lady!"

All this was delivered at about a hundred decibels and every pair of eyes in that room was on me. Normally I would have been bright red and trembling with embarrassment, but not this time. This time my face did not alter its colour at all, but I *was* trembling, only it was with anger, not embarrassment. I'd suddenly had enough of adults telling me off without bothering to listen to any explanation. I looked at her fat scowling face and something inside me snapped.

"I've just about had a gutful of you, Miss Funless Farrant," I yelled at her. "Why don't you just ask why I'm late instead of going off at the deep end? That's typical of you! You only care about your stupid concert. You don't care that three of my best friends have got food poisoning and one of them has had money stolen and the Head won't believe us when we tell her who did it. You don't care that we only took those recorders because we wanted to give you a nice surprise, because I felt sorry for you and thought you'd like another item in the concert. You didn't even bother to listen to us in assembly. Well, I don't want to play in a concert organized by an old frumpy grump like you. It's all so boring, anyway. You'd never think of letting us sing and play things we really enjoy, like 'The Calypso Round', would you? So you can stuff your pathetic concert!"

With that I stomped out of the room, then all the way along the corridor, into the junior cloakroom and into the loos. I went into one of the loos, locked the door, sat down on the lid of the toilet and burst into tears. Once I'd started I couldn't stop. I was crying with frustration and anger and pity. The pity was for Miss Farrant, because although I hated her guts, I couldn't erase from my mind the memory of her bewildered face when I'd delivered my speech.

Eventually, my tears stopped flowing and I began to think what I'd actually done. My heart began to race as I realized that I would be in *big* trouble now. I groaned inwardly and wondered what to do next. I didn't need to wonder for long. There was a gentle tap at the door.

"Leah, is that you? Can I come in?"

It was Andy's voice. I let her in and she squashed on the toilet lid beside me. "Whatever's happened now?" she asked, eyeing my swollen eyes with concern.

So I told her, and to my surprise she laughed. "That's brilliant, Leah. Here was I thinking you'd never say boo to a goose, and all the time you've got the temper of a tigress. I wish I'd been there. I would have just loved to have seen the look on her face…"

"No, you wouldn't, Andy. That's why I'm upset."

"Don't be silly. You gave her exactly what she deserved. What did she say when you'd finished?"

"Nothing. I didn't give her the chance. I just marched out with everyone staring at me as though I'd changed into a frog before their very eyes."

"Oh, Leah!" giggled Andy. I joined in the giggling and we clutched each other helplessly so we wouldn't fall off the loo! If anyone had seen us they would have creased up too. We must have been such a ridiculous sight.

"What did Ms Chambers say after I'd gone?" I asked Andy, as our laughter subsided. "Did she believe you about the ten pounds?"

"She said that unless someone else came to her to say that they'd actually witnessed Barker stealing the money from Jaimini's pocket, she could not assume that what I said was true. It makes me sick, Leah. I'm more determined than ever to nail Barker now. I can't wait to tell Mark the plan after school. I presume I'll be the only one around at the café because the others are ill, and you and Tash will be at the concert rehearsal... Come to think of it, I should be there too, for the choir bit, but still..."

"I'll come to the café with you, Andy. I'm not going to the rehearsal. I've told her she can stuff her stupid concert, and I'm not going back on what I said."

"That means that her choir is going to be short of five people," said Andy.

"No, six," I corrected her, "because I'm going to persuade Tash not to go either."

"And most of the rest of the items are going to suffer, because you're supposed to be playing either the violin, the recorder or the piano in just about everything, aren't you?"

I nodded.

"That means the concert's going to be one big flop," Andy summarized. "And it jolly well serves her right."

I bit my lip.

"Don't start feeling bad about it, Leah. Just remember how horrible she's been to you and the rest of us."

I tried hard to remember, but no matter how hard I tried, I couldn't stop seeing a picture of Miss Farrant's fury crumbling into that sad, bewildered look when I'd told her in no uncertain terms exactly what I thought of her.

Chapter 9

At four-fifteen I was in the kitchen of the café helping Andy and trying with all my might to concentrate on what I was doing. I also kept reminding myself about how great it was going to be getting our revenge on Barker. To tell the truth I was just thinking about anything I possibly could in order to stop remembering where I should really have been.

"There are no extra wages to spare, I'm afraid, Leah," said Jan, with a wink, as she watched me vigorously wiping glasses.

"No, I'm not after more money, honestly."

Jan smiled. "So what is it you're after, then?"

"Andy and I were wondering if we could have a few minutes off to talk to Mark. So we reckoned that if the two of us worked extra hard now, that would make up for the lost time later…"

"Just five minutes off then, but I want to see plenty of hard work first."

So we ceased all chatter and worked our very best and fastest to the accompaniment of Kevin singing "Silence is Golden" which is an old sixties song! We were then free to give Mark a very hurried account of all that had happened since Saturday evening, and to ask him for his help in taking Gary Barker down a peg or two.

Mark listened attentively as we spoke, but he looked grave and doubtful. "Sorry, girls," he said when we'd finished telling him our plan. "Judo doesn't work like that. It's more a form of defence. I can't possibly challenge someone to a fight, when they're not a judo expert."

"Oh, *please*, Mark," we pleaded. "We've been so excited about our plan. Barker wouldn't be able to resist taking up the challenge of a fight with you and it would be so great to see him lose."

"I'd love to teach that bloke a lesson, but not like this, I'm sorry. I'm not prepared to use judo unless I'm severely provoked."

"But you *are* severely provoked."

"No, I'm not. I don't provoke that easily. Sorry girls, forget it."

I suddenly felt utterly drained. I'd pinned all our hopes on Mark helping us, and now we were back to square one. I looked at Andy and saw that her expression was definitely not in the despairing category. In fact she looked positively animated. I know Andy well and I knew she'd got something up her sleeve which she wasn't telling me at the moment.

While she got back to work I went to have a Coke in the café. I'd no sooner been served, than in walked Tash with Fen, Jaimini and Luce. They all looked about a hundred times better than when I'd last seen them.

There was a great deal of chatting at our table as we exchanged stories about our days and our feelings. Luce and Jaimini had got over their negative attitude from earlier on when they didn't have the strength to want revenge on Barker. Now they were feeling better they were all fired up and wanting something to happen. Fen said she would never forgive him for the agony he'd put her through and she'd like to see him well and truly clobbered. So you can imagine it was doubly awful to have to break it to them that Mark wasn't interested in our plan.

I explained to them why Mark wouldn't fight Barker, no matter how cleverly we set up the fight. So that was the end of that. Or so we thought – until guess who came swaggering into the café with his usual entourage? Yes, bragging Barker.

I saw Mark's lips tighten as he went over to take their order. Barker either hadn't noticed us or was deliberately ignoring us, and we were keeping very quiet indeed – just listening and watching.

Andy came out of the kitchen and went up to Mark. "Could you give Kevin a hand, please, Mark?" she asked him. "He's pulled a muscle in his arm and the freezer needs moving out so we can get something that's dropped behind it. It's far too heavy for Jan and me to move."

Mark turned immediately to go and help with the freezer, but he stopped in his tracks at the sound of Barker's voice coming over loud and clear. "Whatever's behind that freezer'll have to stay there until Kevin's injury heals up, I reckon."

Mark turned and walked back to Barker. "What's that supposed to mean?" he asked, in a voice so quiet we only just heard.

"Exactly what it sounds like," sneered Barker. "I've seen Kevin at the gym. He's the only strong guy working in this place."

"So you're saying I'm not strong enough?" Mark asked.

Barker laughed openly at that, and of course that gave his little band of followers the cue to laugh too. I glanced at Andy. She gave me a tentative thumbs-up sign, and I suddenly realized that this whole conversation was going exactly as she'd planned it. So *that* was what she had up her sleeve! Good old Andy. Fancy thinking of such a clever way of getting Barker to provoke Mark.

"I've got an idea," Mark said, icily. "Why don't *you* come and move the freezer, Barker? A tough guy like you should move it in no time at all. It's only three-quarters full at the moment, so it can't weigh more than a quarter of a ton."

Barker was beginning to look the teeniest bit uncomfortable but his friends soon took care of that. "Yeah, show him, Gary. Show him how it's done," they egged him on.

Andy leant over to me, and in a very loud whisper said, "I bet he won't be able to." The rest of us, catching the look in her eye, understood exactly how she wanted us to respond, and said things like, "No chance." "Quite agree."

"It's definitely not worth taking bets on it," continued Andy in another of her famous stage whispers designed to bait Barker.

"Huh!" he retorted loudly. "A tenner says

I'll have the freezer moved in less than a minute without unloading a single thing."

"A tenner says you *won't*," Andy answered him, sticking her chin up determinedly.

"OK, we've all witnessed the bet," Mark said, taking the part of the referee. "Shake on it."

So Andy walked over to Barker, who had stood up. Towering over her, he roughly shook her slim little hand. I couldn't help smiling at the difference in size, although I was worried because you never knew what Barker would do next.

With perfect timing Jan entered the café just as a small crowd of shoppers came in from outside. She hurried over to greet them and help seat them. They were all regulars at the café, and Jan is a firm believer in giving regulars extra special treatment. She was so involved that she didn't notice as Barker, his four friends, Mark and the six of us all went through to the kitchen.

The freezer sat gleaming and solid against the wall. Kevin gaped in amazement at the crowd standing around it. "What the…?"

"It's OK," I whispered. "Barker's about to make a fool of himself, hopefully."

"Oh, good," Kevin whispered back. "What a shame a few of the guys from the gym aren't here to watch. They like him about as much as I like meat flies." And with that observation, he folded his arms and smiled broadly, looking forward to the show. And this was the scene that met Jan's eyes as she came back into the kitchen.

"Why is my kitchen full of customers?" she demanded. "I'm not having it."

"Just a little business to clear up, Jan," Kevin said, putting a restraining hand on her arm. If it had been anyone else but Kevin, Jan wouldn't have put up with it, but she trusted Kevin completely. He could twist her round his little finger.

"Get on with it then, whatever it is," she said, assuming the same stance, arms folded, as Kevin.

"You heard. Get on with it," Mark told Barker, quietly.

Barker rolled up his sleeves and made a big thing of flexing his muscles and breathing deeply. His supporters were shifting their weight self-consciously from foot to foot. We café girls were tense and still, with legs, arms, fingers, all crossed, for good luck.

Barker took the deepest breath ever and gripped the freezer. The veins on his forehead stood out and his whole face quivered as he strained every sinew of his body in the biggest effort I'd ever seen anyone make. He maintained this pose – muscles tense, veins popping out all over the place – as he forced all his weight against the freezer and kept it there for several seconds, then finally fell back exhausted.

Spontaneously, all the onlookers, except the Barker lot, let out their breath.

"It's not over yet," spat Barker, as though we'd all started cheering or something.

He inhaled deeply again and made a noise like a strangled elephant as he threw himself at the unyielding great freezer. Then after a few more seconds of sustained effort, just when he looked as though he was about to burst, he flopped over the freezer from the waist upward, and breathed out noisily.

Jan instantly grabbed Andy, saying, "Come on, back to work, show's over."

"Not quite, it isn't," Andy replied with a gleam in her eye.

"It is as far as I'm concerned," said Jan as she rushed out to hold the fort on her own.

The Barker fans began their feet shuffling routine again, and came out with one or two lame excuses as a gesture to their fallen hero. "It's impossible to move that thing."

"Yeah, it weighs a ton."

"If Barker can't move it, no one can."

Andy strolled up to Barker and held out her hand, palm up. "You owe me ten pounds."

I held my breath. We all did. Very slowly Barker unpeeled himself from the freezer and straightened up. Looking at her as though she was a bit of dirt he said, "That bet was unfair."

"*You* made it."

"No, *you* made it," he practically spat back

at her, "because you knew it was impossible."
Andy didn't flinch or back away. She just
raised her hand a bit closer to his face and
repeated, "You owe me ten pounds." Nobody
else moved a muscle. Barker suddenly relaxed,
folded his arms, and tipping his head to one
side, said, "Tell you what, you can have your
ten pounds if *he* can shift this lump." His
head jerked in Mark's direction but his eyes
never left Andy's face.

"Oh, show him, Mark," came Kevin's
bored-sounding voice, "then we can all get
back to work." Kevin then strolled over to his
Aga as though it wasn't even worth watching,
because Mark moved freezers about all the
time. Personally I was worried because if
Mark rose to the challenge and couldn't do it,
then Andy wouldn't get her tenner. Perhaps
we should draw a halt to the whole thing, here
and now, and simply insist that the bet had
already been won fairly and squarely.

I was about to whisper that to Andy when
Mark put his hands on the freezer and went
through more or less what Barker had just

been through, but with far less fuss and noise. Immediately the freezer moved about ten centimetres and everybody gasped, even Barker himself, whose eyes were nearly popping out of his head. Mark calmly reached down behind the freezer and pulled out a pencil case.

"Thanks, Mark," said Andy. "So stupid of me to drop it down there." I was dying to look at the others, but I didn't want to move my eyes from the action, not even for a second. Barker's friends were really scowling.

"I think you'd better give Andy her ten pounds," Mark said, as he began to walk away. Then something awful happened. We had no time to warn Mark as Barker suddenly lunged at him from behind, but Mark reacted with the speed of lightning. All his judo training suddenly came into play as he threw Barker neatly and swiftly over his shoulder and on to the ground.

And there Barker lay, on his back and looking terrified for the first time ever. His friends began to back away.

"Get up and pay up," said Mark in scarcely more than a whisper. Barker didn't need asking twice. He jumped up, reached into his back pocket, pulled out a ten pound note and handed it to Andy, keeping his eyes on the floor.

"Thank you," said Andy, in a clear bright voice. Then she turned to Jaimini and in the same bright little voice said, "Here you are, Jaimini. This is from Barker."

Well, that made him look up. They all did. But nobody said a word. They just exchanged embarrassed looks as the rest of us smiled in victory. Andy had made her point beautifully. Barker was left in no doubt at all now that we all knew he had stolen Jaimini's ten pound note, but the wonderful thing was, he would never know how we'd found out.

"Let me show you to the door," said Kevin with mock politeness. He made for the back door, not the café door, and opened it. As the red-faced shuffling band of boys went out with Barker bringing up the rear, I heard Kevin say, "And if you *ever* do anything to harm or upset these girls again, you'll have Mark and myself to answer for. Do you hear me?"

Barker nodded like a little child.

"Good," said Kevin, "because the guys at the gym are all buddies of mine." And with that he shut the door and we all let out wild war whoops. Andy flung her arms round Mark's neck, gave him a big kiss and said, "You were fantastic, Mark. That throw was absolutely brilliant!"

Mark winked at her. "I was provoked," he said simply.

"Well, I want to say a big thank you to Andy for setting the whole idea up, and another big thank you to Mark for carrying it out, and another big thank you to Kevin for finishing it off, because now we know we can all relax. Barker wouldn't dare try anything else, now he knows we've got Mark, Kevin and all the guys at the gym to protect us!"

We all clapped and laughed and con-gratulated Jaimini on a great speech, but you know me, there was still the little niggling worry at the back of my mind that Barker would always be a threat.

A few minutes later it was as though nothing had happened. Fortunately the café had been practically empty during out bet, but now it was almost full, so Jan, Mark, Andy and Kevin were all hard at work.

"Don't speak too loudly," Fen said, when we were all round our original table with our Cokes in front of us.

"Why not?" Luce asked.

For answer Fen tipped her head. We glanced over and there was the tape recorder behind the vase of flowers. "Is it on?" Tash asked in a whisper.

"It's been on all the time," Fen answered. "I don't think it will have picked up anything very interesting today though." We all agreed, then Fen suddenly shot up out of her seat.

"I'm supposed to be picking Emmy up from Alice Bainbridge's at five o'clock. I'd better go. Can you ask Andy to take the tape recorder when she finishes?"

"Yes, don't worry. See you tomorrow."

Shortly after that the rest of us split up too. Andy said she was going to be in a rush at six o'clock so I volunteered to take the tape recorder there and then. It was the simplest thing in the world to unplug it and stuff it in my bag without anyone noticing because there was a poster on the wall just above it, advertising a group called Straight Lace who were on tour, so all the others crowded round me and pretended to study the details of the tour.

Tash and I walked part-way home together. "Aren't you worried that you've missed the last rehearsal?" Tash asked me.

"No, are you?"

"A bit," Tash confessed, "but after you told me about Miss Farrant shouting at you and generally being so horrible, yet again, I lost any remaining sense of commitment I may have had." We walked along in silence for a while, both lost in our own thoughts, then Tash said, "It's going to be awful, isn't it?"

"What is?"

"The concert – without you."

"Oh, Tash, stop trying to make me feel guilty. I don't care about it. It's not my problem."

"So aren't you even going to watch the concert?"

"No fear!"

"But what about your parents? Aren't they going?"

"I'm just praying they've forgotten about it. They certainly haven't mentioned it. If they do, I'll just have to tell them the truth. They can't make me go, can they? Anyway, Miss Farrant must have made some other arrangements by now."

"You're joking, Leah. You're the only one who can lead the orchestra. No one else can play that music. It's far too difficult. And then there's the string quartet. She'll have to make it a trio, I suppose."

"It won't work without all four parts. She'll have to play my part herself…" I paused as I began to contemplate the chaos I had caused. Then I heard her voice in my head: "You are getting just a bit too big for your boots if you think you can come breezing in here twenty minutes late, young lady!"

"It's her own fault," I told Tash aggressively. "She should have found out *why* I was late, instead of bawling at me like she did. She's always so hateful and bad-tempered. Today was just the last straw."

"OK, calm down," said Tash.

We parted a few minutes later and I went home to find Kim looking very anxious. "Miss Farrant phoned. She wanted to talk to you. I said I was sorry, I didn't know where you were. She asked me if I'd get you to phone her back at the school when you got in. She said she'd be there all the time leading up to the concert."

"Miss Farrant! Phoned here!"

"What have you been up to, Leah?" Kim asked when she saw the expression on my face.

"I've told Miss Farrant to stuff her concert, that's all."

"That's *all*!" squeaked Kim. "But why?"

"Because she's been horrible to me for weeks and I mean *really* horrible. And to the others. Today was the last straw, so I told her to stuff her concert."

"It doesn't sound like you at all, Leah."

"No, I know it doesn't. So that tells you how impossible she must have been, doesn't it?"

Kim bit her lip and looked worried.

"I'm going to do my homework," I said, going upstairs.

When I got into my room, I realized it was much more tempting to listen to the tape, so I thumbed through a load of old comics and magazines and vaguely listened for a while. It wasn't particularly interesting because it was practically impossible to make out the speech. You could hear a general buzz of chatter, but there was lots of other noise – chairs scraping, cutlery and general thuds and clinks. Then a good deal of that noise seemed to disappear and Jan's voice said, "Let me take that for you … no, that's quite all right. I'll just pop it over here out of your way."

That must have been when we all went into the kitchen, I thought, sitting up a bit. Jan's voice sounded clear as a bell as though she had been standing right over the tape recorder. What if she'd seen it? It would have been terrible. I made a mental note to tell Fen that we really should stop taping things now. It was too risky.

The conversation that the little group of regular customers had had was fairly clear too. One of them was particularly easy to hear. She must have been facing the tape recorder.

"Poor woman," she was saying. I stopped flipping through the magazine and lay on the bed staring at the ceiling and listening. "How long has she known?"

"About three weeks, I guess."

"How bad is it?"

"She's only got a few more months to live, you know."

"It's such a terrible disease, cancer, isn't it?"

"Awful. Absolutely awful. I don't know how she's coped at all…"

"Leah!" This was Kim's voice, yelling up the stairs. I switched off the tape recorder. "Come quickly, I think Stubbles has escaped."

"Oh, no!" I belted downstairs and Kim and I went outside. We each owned a guinea pig. Mine was called Stubbles because his fur was quite rough and stubbly. Kim's was called Candlewick because Kim always thought of original names. Whenever it was fine we put the guinea pigs out in their run to graze in our back garden.

Candlewick was happily nibbling the grass but Stubbles was nowhere to be seen. I reached into the little enclosed bit of their run and felt Stubbles' little body, cold and trembling.

"Oh, Kim, he's ill," I said. I took him out gently and cuddled him against me.

"He's got hypothermia, I think," Kim said. "Bring him into the warm." She put Candlewick in his night-time hutch, loaded him up with plenty of hay, then came in with me and Stubbles. We put him in a cosy box in the airing cupboard.

"I hope he'll be OK," I said, feeling sad. "I couldn't bear it if anything happened to Stubbles."

"He'll be OK," Kim said. "He's probably got a cold like me."

"I didn't know you had a cold."

"A real stinker. I'm going to bed early tonight."

Mum came back in from work then. She gave Stubbles a stroke, then made honey and lemon for Kim and sent her to bed.

"Go and do your homework while I make something to eat," Mum said to me. "Dad'll be home soon."

So I went back up to my room, but it was very difficult to concentrate because I kept thinking about Stubbles. It wasn't till a tear dropped on to my science book and smudged my work on The Big Bang, that I realized how sad I was feeling.

Our meal was a very quiet one. I kept leaving the table to see how Stubbles was getting on. He was just beginning to feel warmer, thank goodness. Dad felt him and said he was certain he'd be all right. I didn't eat much because I wasn't at all hungry. Mum thought I might be going down with the same thing that Kim had got, but I just felt sad. I couldn't stop thinking about that poor woman that those customers had been talking about on the tape. I mean, here was I worrying about a guinea pig and that poor woman was dying of cancer.

I went upstairs and pressed the PLAY button, then flopped on the bed to listen. What I heard next shocked me to the core.

"It must be tiring teaching music full time, mustn't it?"

"Yes, especially when you're carrying all that weight around. She's also put on a lot more because of the treatment, you know."

"Poor thing…"

"Still, she can relax a bit more after tonight when the concert's over."

I shot up and covered my mouth with my hand. I suddenly felt sick.

"I don't think she's going to finish off the term, you know, so let's hope the concert's a great success so she can go out on a high!"

"I'm sure it will be. She speaks so well of the children at school."

"It's Cableden Comp., isn't it?"

"Yes, and apparently she's got some very musical students there, so I hope they do her proud tonight."

My world seemed to collapse around me for a moment, then I shot up off my bed, ran downstairs, grabbed Mum and said, "Concert! Quick!"

"Oh, the concert!" screeched Mum. "I'd forgotten all about it. Hurry up Stu, it's Leah's school concert."

My watch said seven-twenty-one and the concert was due to start at seven-thirty. I got on the phone to Andy while Mum was getting her coat and bag.

"Andy, urgent! Phone the others! You *must* come to the concert. I've just found out that Miss Farrant's got cancer. This concert is her final one … EVER…" My voice began to crack but I pulled myself together because time was running out. "See you soon. Bye."

Then I grabbed my violin and music, called

out "bye" to Kim, who was in bed but not asleep, and we all piled into the car and roared off to school.

Chapter 10

Why is it that when you're in a tearing hurry every traffic light is against you? There's only one ordinary set of lights between us and the school, but there are lots of roadworks at the moment and we had to wait ages at those lights. I was sitting tense and worried in the back counting the seconds, and guessing how many it would take before it changed to amber.

The conversation I'd heard on the tape was playing loud and clear in my head and with every word my sadness weighed me down a little bit more. Then the final angry speech I'd flung at Miss Farrant came into my mind, and the guilt came piling up on my sadness. I strained to see the car clock in the front – seven-twenty-eight.

The concert was due to start in two minutes, but how could it start? The programme had already been printed. I was in almost every item and most of the items didn't make sense without my part. The recorder piece would be all right and the choir... No it wouldn't – not with six of us missing. So many people had left the choir that there were only fourteen remaining. Without us six it just wouldn't work.

Oh, hurry up Andy, hurry up everybody. We must make this concert work. I clutched the car seat and sat forward, my seat-belt pressing into my leg. Then a picture of Stubbles came into my mind. My sweet little guinea pig that lay snuggled up in the lovely warm airing cupboard because he'd got a cold. And for a moment earlier on I'd thought I'd lost him. I'd thought he was dying. Oh, Miss Farrant, if only I'd known. Mrs Merle's words flashed into my head – "Don't be too hard on Miss Farrant. She can't help the way she is … at the moment."

"We're here, Leah. Get ready to jump out."

"I'm ready, don't worry."

I ran up the path to the main entrance while Mum and Dad went to park the car. I flew down the corridor and flung open the door to the auditorium and belted in. Then I stopped in confusion. The door had banged against the wall and stuck as usual, so every member of the audience had turned round to see who could be so noisy and insensitive when the concert had already started. Because it had.

Miss Farrant was making the welcoming speech. She stood in the middle of the stage with the tiny orchestra behind her. Where I should have been sitting there was an empty chair. It was as though she was expecting me. There was no need to put a chair out for me, yet she had done.

"…some of the items will have to be omitted…" she was saying. But she stopped talking when I crashed in, and we looked at each other from opposite ends of the hall. Her face was calm and accepting, no trace of cross-ness. For a moment there was total silence in that auditorium, then we both spoke together, the same words.

"I'm sorry…"

Miss Farrant broke into a smile, a lovely warm welcoming smile, and held out her hand to me. I walked in a kind of daze up the aisle and up the steps to the stage. She met me at the top of the steps. I gave her my best smile back and tried to find some words but there was something in my throat that was stopping me speaking. I could feel tears pricking the backs of my eyes. I sat down in my place.

Turning back to the audience, who were wide-eyed and attentive, she spoke in a jokey way. "Well, you can draw a line straight through my last speech and I'll start again."

The audience laughed in relief that the atmosphere had lightened. But Miss Farrant couldn't continue because the door opened again, a little more quietly this time, and in crept Mum and Dad followed by Andy, Fen and Tash. And surprise surprise, there was Jan as well. I wondered fleetingly whether she'd brought Andy and the others in her car. They sat down at the back.

"Oh, good, three more members of the choir. Come and sit at the front, girls." Andy looked round to check Miss Farrant was definitely addressing them. She obviously couldn't believe these new kindly tones. I gave her an encouraging nod and they came forward cautiously as though Miss Farrant might at any moment change into a monster and leap on them. When they were almost at the front, in came Luce and Jaimini with their parents and Luce's younger brothers.

"And now we are complete!" beamed Miss Farrant with her hands clasped in front of her. "Come straight to the front Jaimini and Lucy." Jaimes and Luce made the same careful approach as the other three had. They also sat down with the rest of the choir.

"Right, I think you're going to enjoy this evening's concert. You may notice one or two changes in the programme – or even nine or ten changes – but who cares!"

The audience laughed and so did the orchestra. Miss Farrant turned round and gave us a broad wink. It's going to be all right, I thought. It's just about going to be all right.

There was a special feeling amongst the players in the orchestra that evening. It was as though the others sensed that it was import- ant to do our very best for Miss Farrant on this occasion. We played two pieces and the audience clapped and clapped at the end. Miss Farrant made me stand up and take a special bow of my own because I was the leader.

"Right, it's the choir next," she announced, "but we're not going to sing any of the items on the programme. We're going to sing you a special favourite of this choir's – 'The Calypso Round'."

I couldn't believe my ears. All the choir were looking at each other and grinning from ear to ear. And boy did we sing! I don't know how the school remained standing, our singing was so strong. Miss Farrant was practically dancing, she was conducting with such vigour, and for the last minute of the song, the audience clapped in time with the strong rhythm. It was absolutely magic.

And so it went on. Item after item of our favourite pieces. And when the little wind group played, Mr Osbourne, who I'd always thought was nothing but a boring science teacher, joined in on the trumpet. He improvised jazz just like a professional player, bringing the music to life. The audience clapped louder than ever and called out "Encore!" wanting more and more.

Miss Farrant looked so hot and tired, yet she conducted and played the piano as though she was the fittest, healthiest person in the room. It wasn't a long concert, but it was an action-packed, wonderful one, and when it came to an end it was obvious the audience wanted more.

"If I may address you briefly," Miss Farrant said to the audience as she took centre stage once more. "Some of you already know that I'm leaving this school due to my ill health." The audience looked shocked and saddened. "I was going to try and hang on till the end of term, but Ms Chambers has very kindly released me as from the end of tonight's concert." Again a wave of despondency swept the audience and the pupils. "I know you'll all be happy to learn that Mrs Merle will be taking my place. And if she's anything like as good as her brother, Mr Osbourne, this school is going to have a superb music department!"

I saw Luce clap her hand to her mouth, which made her big eyes look even bigger, staring at me in surprise at this revelation. "Brother!" we mouthed at one another, then fell into helpless giggles, which didn't matter because the audience were clapping in appreciation of Mr Osbourne.

"There's just one more item to come," Miss Farrant went on. "It's a recorder piece written by Leah Bryan for her friends. This is a very special piece by a very special young lady, that's why I've saved it till last. Leah is a typical artist. She's impulsive, impatient and at times impossible! Just like me. We're both 'imps'!" The audience roared with laughter and I giggled at the thought of being a fellow imp with Miss Farrant.

Then her face took on a more serious expression. "This piece that we're about to hear from Leah and her friends is going to mark a high spot for me. The whole concert is being taped, so I'll have the pleasure, time and time again, of listening to this evening's wonderful music, but I think that most of all I shall treasure the memory of what we're about to hear… Leah's Piece."

She smiled as she handed us six school recorders, and we took our places in a line at the front of the stage. I counted us in, and we played. I don't know how I managed to play. It took all my concentration to stop myself bursting into tears. Over and over again I thought, Thank goodness I found out in time.

The applause at the end was deafening and we stood there smiling at each other and at the audience for what felt like about five minutes but it was probably more like twenty seconds. Ms Chambers made a lovely speech about Miss Farrant and presented her with a huge bouquet. I wished I could make the evening last a bit longer as I watched Miss Farrant's happiness. "Thank goodness we came," Andy whispered to me. "How did you find out?"

"From the tape. Those regulars in the café were discussing it… If only we could prolong the evening a bit, Andy."

Andy must have passed this along the row to Fen who was on the end, because this message came back to me a few seconds later. "Fen's going to ask Jan."

"Going to ask Jan what?"

"If she'll open up the café."

Sure enough there was Fen talking to Jan. I couldn't see the expression on Jan's face but she suddenly stood up and gave me a thumbs-up sign. Then she carried on making a few more signs and gestures which I took to mean "Tell Miss Farrant to come to the café". Fen came rushing up to me to confirm this excitedly. "Jan says Miss Farrant and the other teachers who are here are welcome to come to the café."

I passed this on to Ms Chambers, and when all the audience had trooped out, and there were only we six pupils, some of our parents, Jan and the few teachers left, Ms Chambers clapped her hands and made an important announcement that Miss Farrant was to be the guest of honour at a surprise party at *The Café*, by special invitation of Fenella Brooks' Aunt Jan! Everybody cheered and we set off in various cars.

As soon as we got to the café, the six of us set to work with Jan, building a party atmosphere. We blew up balloons and hung streamers. We then rushed round pouring out drinks for everyone and handing round crisps and nuts and other nibbles.

When I handed Ms Chambers a glass of wine, she said, "I'd like to have a quick word with you and Agnès, Leah." I went to get Andy, thinking, Oh please, don't say anything that will spoil this lovely atmosphere, Ms Chambers.

"I just wanted you both to know that with the help of Miss Farrant, who trusts you implicitly Leah, I have got to the bottom of this business with Gary Barker. It seems he is definitely responsible for contaminating Lucy's sausage rolls and for taking the ten-pound note. I grilled Gary's friends and then Gary himself, and he has finally confessed to his crimes. He will be suspended, of course, and I shall make sure he pays Jaimini back."

"He already has done." And we told Ms Chambers all about the freezer-shifting competition, which made her giggle in a way I didn't think head teachers *could* giggle!

"Oh, and Leah," she added as I was just about to go and top up a few drinks, "I'm glad you came tonight. The concert wouldn't have been the same without you."

Miss Farrant approached me next, so I put down my tray of drinks and we sat down together at one of the tables.

"I'm so glad you decided not to desert me, in the end."

I went pink. "You see ... I didn't realize..."

I began awkwardly.

"I knew you'd come in the end – even when you didn't phone the school."

Miss Farrant and I chatted for ages. I told her about my guinea pig and she told me about the pet guinea pig she used to have when she was a child. She spoke so lovingly about it that I asked her why she didn't have one now. She laughed her head off when I suggested she get herself one. "You know Leah, you look at life in such an interesting way, but you're absolutely right. Just because I'm a fusty old lady it shouldn't stop me from having a guinea pig!"

We decided she could share mine and she said she'd be round at the weekend to introduce herself to Stubbles. I told her all about our café work and she promised to pop into the café regularly, for as long as she could. I bit my lip and looked down because we hadn't really talked about her cancer.

"I think you know I haven't got very long to live Leah, but I also want you to know that because of you, I'm really going to enjoy whatever time I've got left. You gave me such a shock when you put me in my place earlier on today. And it was just what I needed to make me stop in my tracks and have a really good think and a jolly good talk to myself.

"I didn't see the point of living when I was told I'd got cancer, because there didn't seem anything to live for. I found myself resenting people who were lucky enough to live normal lives. So if any one of these lucky people stepped out of line, in any way whatsoever, it made me hopping mad – as you know! As for your piece, I heard every note the first time you played it. It really moved me, but I thought that if I once gave way to my real feelings, I'd lose the tough shell I'd built around me to protect myself. I know it's hard for you to understand all this…"

"I understand," I told her quietly.

"A toast to Miss Farrant," announced Jan, banging a spoon on the table.

Everyone raised their glasses and said, "To Miss Farrant!" Then we all broke into "For she's a jolly good fellow."

Finally, after much chinking of glasses and toasting of just about everybody in the room, the party split up. Jan said she'd clear up in the morning, but Ms Chambers said, "Not a bit of it! You can't do all this work on your own when you've been kind enough to let us have the party here. No, on this one occasion, I give these girls permission to come into school in morning break which means they can come and help here first."

"Yes!" we all said, punching the air with our fists.

I sat on my bed at home thinking what a day it had been. Full of sadness, happiness, fear, guilt, panic, you name it! I knew it would take me ages to get to sleep that night. There was too much buzzing around in my head. I went downstairs and looked at Stubbles. He was warm and bright-eyed. He whistled at me and snuggled into my neck when I picked him up. He then munched his way through a very large carrot at high speed, so I popped him back in his night-time hutch with Candlewick who was delighted to see him.

Back in my bedroom, I suddenly remembered something. I opened my bedroom window and called across our back garden in a loud whisper, "Hey Stubbles, someone's coming to see you at the weekend. I think you'll like her... I do."

As I shut the window I heard Kim calling me faintly from her room. I must have woken her up. I went in and sat on the edge of her bed.

"How did you know someone was coming at the weekend?" she asked in a very sleepy voice.

"I meant Miss Farrant," I told her softly.

"Oh... I thought you meant Oliver, because he's coming too," she said, then rolled on to her other side.

"What! Oliver?" I said, rather too loudly for a sleeping house. "Are you sure? Coming here?"

"Yes. He phoned while you were at the concert. They're coming to stay the weekend with us."

"Brilliant!" I cried.

Kim did a big yawn as she said the next words, so I only just heard them.

"They're moving to Cableden."

"To Cableden… Mega brilliant!" I breathed, smiling into the darkness.

Join

Would you and your friends like to know more about Fen, Tash, Leah, Andy, Jaimini and Luce?

We have produced a special bookmark to commemorate the launch of the Café Club series. To get yours free, together with a special newsletter about Fen and her friends, their creator, author Ann Bryant, and advance information about what's coming next in the series, write (enclosing a self-addressed label, please) to:

The Café Club
c/o the Publicity Department
Scholastic Children's Books
Commonwealth House
1-19 New Oxford Street
London WC1A 1NU

We look forward to hearing from you!